Tal

About The Author 1
Chapter One 2
Chapter Two 14
Chapter Three 30
Chapter Four 47
Chapter Five 64
Chapter Six 86
Chapter Seven 114
Chapter Eight 128
Chapter Nine 143
Chapter Ten 150

AMANDA'S MARK
OR
I ACCIDENTALLY CALLED MY BOSS MOM

The Sampson Saga, Book One

Deep Rest

For and to my wife, A, of which this is a letter and labor of love. Rawr, XD, and such.

Patreon.com/DeepRestWriting[1]

Copyright © 2024 by Deep Rest

Second Edition

All rights reserved. No part of this publication may be reproduced, stored, or transmitted in any form or by any means, electronic, mechanical, photocopying, recording, scanning, or otherwise without written and verified permission from the author. It is illegal to copy this book, post it to a website, or distribute it by any other means without permission.

• • • •

This edition is a collection of the I Accidentally Called My Boss Mom story parts one through ten, assembled and edited for copyright and distribution purposes. This book is a work of fiction. Names, characters, businesses, organizations, places, and events are either a product of the author's imagination or are used fictitiously. Any resemblance to actual persons, living or dead, events or locales is purely coincidental.

Also by the author:
How To Be A Trophy Husband Act I
The Deep Rest Anthology Volume I

• • • •

Edited by:
The Nerdy Siren
Produced by:
BitchCraft
The Freaky Doc
The Nerdy Siren
Noctu
Book Cover illustrated by NOV32

---

1. http://patreon.com/DeepRestWriting

About The Author

Deep Rest is a self-published author who writes serialized erotic romance. In high school, he was dissuaded from pursuing writing as a passion due to creating disturbing and unwelcome horror fiction as a result of undiagnosed ADHD, depression, and a particularly perturbing domestic violence incident. Ten years later, he impulsively cut his teeth with the story 'I Accidentally Called My Boss Mom' - originally posted free to read on Reddit. It was written on a whim after he read a satisfactory smut story and thought - *I could write something at least as good as this.*

Part One received unforeseen and explosive acclaim and, along with Part Two, garnered more than a million collective views within two weeks. All ten parts, almost fifty thousand words, were posted for free the following month. He began a Patreon campaign - Deep Rest Writing- to let Patrons read the rough drafts of every chapter, as well as view the documents being written in real-time. Since achieving cult success, Deep Rest continues what is now called The Sampson Saga with Book Two: How To Be A Trophy Husband, currently being written and posted for free. Deep Rest survives in Oklahoma, the armpit of the United States, and supports his wife, mother-in-law, brother-in-law, three cats, and a dog that is basically a cat.

Chapter One

Being an office temp is better than flipping burgers, I suppose. I'm twenty years old, and I skipped out on college, so my options are limited. I started this new job four weeks ago. I had to get a suit from Goodwill, fill out a proper resume, and endure a tense interview with the department director I was to work for. She introduced herself as Amanda Jones, and I had never met a more beautifully intimidating woman in my entire life.

She was slightly shorter than me, about 5'8", but her presence was intense. She was significantly older than me, probably thirty-eight, and aging gracefully. She wore a modest black knee-length dress and wore her hair down to her shoulders, with deep bangs cut short just above her eyes. It was very nearly black but glowed red when the sun shone through. She had Business Goth down to a T.

Her face was carved like a Roman statue, neutral yet serious. She studied me with deep brown eyes, and I couldn't hold eye contact with her for more than a few seconds.

She made me nervous to my core. No one had ever had this effect on me, and it was terrifying. Thankfully, once I was hired, I could relax a bit and not be under her scrutiny any longer. She gave orders to the manager, Gordon, who gave orders to me. Gordon was a nice man in his fifties. The kind of guy you know has an immaculate lawn. He set me up at a small corner desk surrounded by reams of paper tucked away in a forgotten area of the office floor.

My main job would be digitizing physical documents and shredding them. My other main job would be to walk from cubicle to cubicle and receive coffee orders. I was an office bitch. It beat being stuck in a hot kitchen, breathing grease all day, though.

Over the next few days, I got into the rhythm of my job. Every morning, I would get coffee orders, except for Amanda's, since she preferred to make her own in the comfort of her office. Then, I'd get to work digitizing and shredding. It was quite dull, over and over, running paper through the scanner and then the shredder. Every few hours, Gordon would come by and shoot the shit for a few minutes, sipping on his black coffee. It wasn't until Friday afternoon that I made my first mistake.

Gordon had come by to check on me. "Hey Mark, have you managed to get through 86 yet?"

"I finished it a few hours ago," I replied. "I decided I wanted to clean up this corner close to the desk so I could have some more room. I'm halfway through 2016 right now."

His expression changed. "Did you... Shred 2016?"

My heart rate increased. "Yes."

He nodded slightly. "Alright, we'll need to go tell Amanda." He turned and began maneuvering across the floor towards her office.

I didn't know what I had done wrong. I stood up, adjusted the wrinkles out of my suit, and followed Gordon. He stopped outside her office and motioned for me to stay put. He went inside, and I stood, wracking my brain about why 2016 would be significant. Soon, he left her office.

"It'll be alright!" He said cheerily as he patted my shoulder. Then, he motioned for me to go inside. I gulped and opened her office door.

I walked inside her office and stood beside two leather chairs before her sizeable wooden desk. She was sitting regally on a distressed leather chair, tapping away at a laptop. When she looked up at me, my heart leaped into my throat. My heart raced as I met her eyes, and my breathing changed as my throat became painful from the anxiety of the situation.

"Mr. Sampson, did you shred 2016?" She asked directly.

"Yes, ma'am," I said slowly.

She waited, but I gave no excuse or meek explanation. "We need to keep physical copies of those documents from the current day back ten years. Gordon hadn't told you since you weren't close to 2014 yet."

"Oh," I whispered.

How is she doing this to me?

She noticed my discomfort. "It's fine, really. You'll need to print out what you shredded and refile it, " she said comfortingly.

"Yes, ma'am." I blurted, relieved, starting towards the door.

"Mr. Samp—" She stopped, then continued gently. "Mark, until you get the hang of things around here, don't do anything unless someone tells you to, okay?"

"Yes, Mom. Thank you, Mom." I squeaked.

What the fuck??

"I mean! Ma'am! Thank you." I stammered. "S- S-Sorry."

When I looked up at her, her eyebrows furrowed, and she looked puzzled. She studied me intently. After a few moments, she nodded toward the door and returned to her laptop. I left quickly, mortified by what I had just said. I navigated back to my desk, where I sat for the rest of the day, fixing my mistake and thinking about how I called my boss, Mom.

After work, I rushed home to change and went to the gym, desperately looking for my gym crush. My crush would distract me from whatever I was feeling towards Amanda, but she didn't show. My workout was subsequently deflated and short-lived.

The following day, after I had delivered coffee to my grateful coworkers, Gordon notified me that Amanda wanted to see me in her office. I was crushed. She wasn't going to let it go. I made my way to her office, but when I opened the door, she acted like it had never happened. In fact, she seemed quite pleasant and happy.

"Good morning, Mark." She said. "Please, sit down."

"Yes, Ma'am."

She gestured to one of the leather chairs in front of her desk. She had moved them to face each other. I quickly sat down. She walked absentmindedly over to her coffee machine on a table against her office wall. She pressed a button and dispensed coffee into two pristine white cups. I used this opportunity to take a good look at her.

Good fucking god.

Today, she wore a black skirt, which was shorter than the dress she wore to my interview. It framed her perfect ass like a picture. Her legs were toned and sculpted. She had on a business casual white blouse, and it accentuated her breasts without showing cleavage. It took me a second to realize she had no shoes on. She'd been barefoot when I walked in. She took the coffees from the machine and walked back over, handing me one before sitting in the other chair and crossing her legs. She bounced her leg lazily on her knee, and I saw she had all-black nail polish on her toes.

I realized I was staring at her feet a little too long.

Since when are you into feet?

I looked up at her face, and she had a slight grin.

"Do you like it?" She asked.

"Yes," I whispered hoarsely.

"The coffee, Mark." She giggled.

Idiot.

I looked down at the coffee. "Right."

I took a sip. It tasted incredible. I cleared my throat. "This is so good! Where is it from?"

"A little town in Mexico." She put her coffee down on the desk.

"Mark, if you're going to stay here, I'd like to get to know you better. You're not required to answer, but if you do, please answer honestly, " she said seriously.

I put my coffee down and nodded.

"Why would you want to work in a boring office like this?" She said amusingly.

Are you gonna be honest?

"Uh." I swallowed and took a breath. "I partied quite a bit when I was younger, and I'm done with it now. I'm trying to start my life seriously, and this is as good a place as any to start." I finished with a nod.

She nodded, accepting my answer as true, although it seemed she didn't care either way. Her eyes darted and quickly met mine before she spoke.

"Are you in a serious relationship?"

Why does she care about that?

"No...I ended things with my high school girlfriend when she went to college; I didn't want to get dragged along since I had to work full time."

Before I looked down from her eyes, I glimpsed her smile slightly while she casually undid the top button of her blouse and pretended to stretch her arm.

My heart, already racing from being alone with her, went even faster.

"Do you like working here?"

I shrugged. "It's better than flipping burgers, and it leaves me enough energy to hit the gym after work."

"Do you lift weights often?"

I nodded. "I grew up very skinny, but in the last few years, I've managed to put on forty pounds, most of it muscle. Now I'm around two hundred pounds."

She smiled. "Congratulations. How strong are you? You look strong." She said with a smirk.

"Well, I could probably pick you up easily, Ma'am," I said softly.

She raised an eyebrow, then suddenly uncrossed her legs and began to stand up, reaching for the coffee cups.

"H-Here, let me." I stammered and jumped up, grabbing the coffee cups and walking to the machine.

I got us refills, and when I turned around, I saw that she had unbuttoned the second button of her blouse. Standing, I had a better angle of her cleavage and saw she was wearing a lacy white bra.

I must've passed the test.

After I had sat down, she leaned forward, giving me a fantastic view. "I need a personal assistant. Is that something you're interested in?"

"Absolutely, Ma'am. I'd do anything for you, Ma'am."

She giggled. Her laughter was like Heaven's choir.

"Good boy." She said slyly.

Blood surged like a tsunami to my groin. I was instantly erect, and sitting down combined with these suit pants let me hide none of it. She reclined back in her chair and didn't hide the fact that she was staring at my waist.

Fuck.

I was rock hard, and there was nothing I could do. Amanda gave me an out, though. She stood and walked back behind her desk.

"Finish out what you're doing today, get coffee in the morning, and then we'll discuss your ..." She paused, leaning on her desk, and dragged a finger across her lips. "Position."

Fuck it.

I stood from the chair, and my cock nearly burst my zipper. Her eyes widened as she stared at it.

"Yes, Ma'am. Thank you, Ma'am," I said hurriedly, my courage rapidly fading. I spun and made for the door.

I paused before opening the door, took a breath, and walked out. Thankfully, no one was near her office. I adjusted myself so it wasn't quite as noticeable and quickly made my way back to my desk.

The next few hours were a blur. I had no idea what was happening to me. No woman I'd ever been with had made me feel like this. I didn't understand it. Was she just fucking with me? I'd been with several girls before and knew enough to flirt, but this felt like something else. Something animalistic.

Among other things, Gordon had me package the 2023 files and ship them off to the company attorney. I was scrambled in my thoughts and feelings. I couldn't focus. Just the image of Amanda was making my brain melt away. I was in a state of euphoria and tortured with worry at the same time. Then, I saw my second mistake. And this was a big one. On my desk, a box with big, bold letters:

2023 COMPLETE DOCUMENTATION

I'm going to fucking kill myself.

My heart sank, and my throat began to close up. My hands started shaking, my stomach curdled, and I thought I might lose my lunch. My eyes began to get red, and I had to blink back tears. I let her down.

This isn't something you can fix or hide. You have to tell her.

I started speed-walking toward Amanda's office. Gordon was at his desk as I approached, looking at me quizzically.

"I fucked up." I mouthed silently.

I stood at her door and knocked once. She told me to enter.

I walked in and shut the door behind me. She saw my expression and was beautifully concerned. It took everything in me not to break down crying.

"I... I ... shipped the 2003 documents, not the 2023 documents." I whispered, my voice faintly cracking. "I'm so sorry. What can I do? What do I need to do?"

Amanda looked at me with a strange expression. Then, her face was calmly accepting. She gestured towards the leather chair. I walked towards it, standing above it. I couldn't stop shaking. She stood up and quietly walked over to the door. I heard the lock click. I felt her walk behind the chair I was standing in front of. Her hands caressed my shoulders.

"You—" She gently pushed down on my shoulders, my knees gave way, and I collapsed into the chair.

"Need to relax," she finished.

She leaned over the back of the chair, her breasts falling heavy on my shoulders. She whispered into my ear.

"Mommy will fix it."

Oh.

I was hard instantly. I could feel my heartbeat throbbing in my cock. Just one word and I felt precum trickle out of my tip, smearing into my underwear.

Amanda stood up, gracefully walked behind her desk, and snatched her cell phone. Quickly, she walked towards the window and began speaking in a low voice with someone. The conversation lasted only thirty seconds. As soon as it was over, she hung up, twirled around, and gazed at me with concern.

She moved back toward me; every step she took was slow and deliberate. I could barely perceive each step; it was like she floated through the air. Eventually, she moved in front of the desk directly in front of where I sat and perched gently on it.

"When was the last time you came?"

"Um." I blushed.

She bent over, her cleavage placed directly beneath her face, and reached her hand out to lift my chin with two fingers. I peered into her eyes as she brushed her thumb across my bottom lip and saw no malice.

Can you really trust her? She's your boss.

"I—" I swallowed. I took a deep breath and decided to let go.

"I haven't cum in two weeks, Ma'am." I whimpered.

She smiled with so much affection that it radiated like sunlight from her face. She extended her leg, and before I could comprehend, her foot fell into my lap. Her heel rested on my balls, and the ball of her foot put gentle pressure against my shaft. I felt lighting strike down my spine, through my groin, and out the tip of my cock. A moan escaped my lips, and I smacked my hand to my face, covering my mouth in shock.

"Shhhh." She whispered. "You really don't have a nice young woman taking care of this?"

I shook my head no while she moved her foot up and down against me. She put more pressure at the base and slid up, eased the pressure, and slid back down. She was milking it, causing a steady stream of precum to collect near my waistband.

"That's a shame. From what I can feel, the girls in this town are missing out." She said coyly.

She pulled her leg back, stood up, and then moved to the side, quickly snatching something I couldn't see from her desk.

"Stand up."

I took my hand from my face and stood, my dick straining against my pants, begging to be released.

She leaned her hip on the desk beside me, one hand behind her back. She was staring at my package. She glanced up at me and gestured to my pants.

Do it.

I slowly unbuckled, then pulled my pants and underwear down just past my waist in one smooth motion.

My cock sprang up so hard it smacked my stomach before standing straight out. It wasn't anything too impressive, but I was proud of it. A solid six inches long, circumcised, and at least two inches thick. It seemed thicker, given how long it had been since I had cum. It had several large veins running down its length, trying to burst through my skin. It bobbed up and down with every heartbeat, and the tip glistened with precum.

Amanda's eyes turned into saucers. She licked her lips, seemed to contemplate something, then decided against it. She set her face neutral and slowly walked behind me.

"Lean forward and put your hands on the table."

I obeyed instantly. I didn't care how strange the situation was, I just needed to cum. She could've breathed in my direction at this point, and I would've exploded.

She stood directly behind me and suddenly wrapped her free hand around my abdomen, traveling up my shirt, feeling my abs, and then dragging her nails down them. She stopped with her palm flattened on my lower stomach, just before my crotch. Her touch nearly made me collapse, and I set all my weight on my hands, my legs unable to support my body.

She leaned into me, pressing her breasts into my back. "You need to cum for Mommy." She purred.

My cock spasmed, and she whirled her other hand around my body. She was fully embracing me now. Her words made me shoot a rope of precum, and miraculously, her other hand held a whiskey glass, depositing my precum in the bottom.

What is happening–

Her hand on my stomach moved down, then slid up the length of my cock, and gripped it tight. Her thumb caressed the tip, gliding freely in circles, slippery from my cum. The sensation made me moan uncontrollably, and I clenched.

"Relax and push," she whispered.

I slowly forced myself to unclench, held my breath, and pushed like I was peeing. Slowly I began to freely flow precum into the glass, pouring out of my cock while she played with the tip. I pushed as long as I could, willing the precum into the glass, but soon, I gasped and had to take a breath.

"You're doing so good, sweetie." She cooed. "Now."

She let go, dipped her fingers into the glass, then lathered it onto my dick. Suddenly, she started stroking, gaining speed.

"Ohhh fuuucckkkk." I whimpered, feeling it boiling inside me.

As she stroked, my body started to shudder and convulse. I began to hyperventilate, and my heart was pounding through my chest. It was heaven and hell all at once. I needed it to end, but I couldn't let it stop. I was at the precipice, floating at the edge of limbo, but I needed a push.

"Cum." She commanded with the voice of God.

I spilled everything of myself into the glass, flooding it with semen. I came and came and came, shoving a fist into my mouth to keep from screaming. My body jerked and writhed as it forced my cum out. I removed my fist from my mouth and breathed a huge sigh of relief as it began to subside.

My dick grew smaller but kept twitching, still sensitive to Amanda's touch.

"Good boy!" She exclaimed sweetly and kissed me on the cheek.

She let go of my dick and pulled her body around me to lean on the desk. I watched her staring at me with hunger in her eyes as she raised the whiskey glass. It was over a third full of my milky white cum. Before I could say anything, she raised it to her lips, tipped the glass, and slid all of my cum down her throat.

"I... You... That was ..." I stuttered, unable to form a complete thought or sentence.

"Do you know what that was?" She asked, licking her lips.

I shook my head.

"That was an ownership ritual, sweetie." She whispered, leaning forward; her mouth paused before touching my lips.

"You belong to me now."

She kissed me, her tongue slipping past my teeth and invading my mouth. I sucked her tongue greedily, trying to taste her and myself.

She pulled away and smiled. I grinned back.

She turned and briskly walked toward the office wall. Pushing on a panel, the wall gave way, revealing a secret bathroom. She disappeared inside for a minute, then returned with a washcloth. She reached down and cleaned me. The washcloth was pleasantly warm and soft, causing me to slip a little moan.

"I... Um." I stammered, pulling my pants up after she was finished. "Well, that was fucking intense. But if you, um, own me... I mean, what if I... Am I not allowed to—"

"I'm not threatened by girls, Mark." She cut me off. Her expression was territorially playful. "Because ultimately, you belong to me."

That's clear as mud.

"Yes, Ma'am."

She smiled. She walked behind her desk, opened a drawer, and retrieved two business cards and a black metal credit card. She handed them to me.

"Tomorrow, start your work day by visiting my personal hairdresser first. Tell her I sent you, she knows what I like. Second, visit this tailor and get a suit worth at least five grand. No more of this." She gestured at my Goodwill Special.

"Last, pick up the office coffee order. I'm sure you know it by heart now."

I nodded. "Yes, Ma'am".

"And?"

"Thank you, Mommy."

As I exited her office, Gordon looked up from his desk with concern.

"Damn, Mark. She gave you the business, didn't she?" He said, frowning.

"Yeah, man." I shrugged. "But it's definitely better than flipping burgers."

Chapter Two

I woke up Friday morning, showered, located the cards Amanda gave me, and was on my way. My first stop was the hairdresser. I pulled up to the shop in my beat-up daily driver and immediately felt out of place. This was a place for rich people, not me. The sign was gold, the floor marble, the seats leather, and the people wealthy. I took a breath, calmed my nerves, and strode inside the double doors. The receptionist was front and center at a large counter. I walked up and asked for Miranda. She gave me a dumbfounded look but pointed me to the back left corner of the shop. There, a thick and curvy woman with bright yellow hair was waiting. I walked through and introduced myself.

"Hi, I'm Mark. Amanda told me that you know what she wants me to look like," I said without hesitation.

Miranda looked taken aback for a second, then studied me. "Really ..." She said wistfully. She looked me up and down, then smiled wickedly before quickly biting her lip. After a few moments, she chuckled. "I guess she found what she was looking for." She said in a measured tone.

I smiled faintly.

Am I a fantasy for Amanda that she finally gets to act on?

Miranda clapped her hands together. "Right! Let's make you perfect." She said seductively.

Miranda was thicker and deceptively beautiful. Her features were rounded, her eyes strikingly blue, and her breasts and butt curvy and plump. Once she sat me down in the chair, she ensured I knew she could play the game. She gave me lingering touches, dragged her large breasts against me, and made pointed comments whenever she noticed a tent forming at my waist.

She designed my hair to be cut shorter on the bottom with a longer flow at the top. It didn't seem like she did much work, as most of the time was spent flirting with me, but I looked completely different.

"Okay, here's your new style. Keep it this way daily so that it starts flowing like this naturally." She demanded.

"Thank you so much. It looks incredible, really." I stood up, taken aback by myself in the mirror.

"It looks incredible because it's on you, pretty boy." She winked and moved past me, brushing her ass against my crotch deliberately. I thanked her and paid using Amanda's card.

"I'll make Amanda send you to me again soon." She said mischievously.

"Be careful what you wish for," I said, flirting back. She faked looking shocked, smiled, then shooed me off.

The next stop was the suit place, which was decidedly less fun. I spent an hour being measured by a grumpy older man and another waiting for the suit to be tailored. I finally managed to escape with a sharp grey suit and red shirt, and I opted not to get a tie. Since I was only going to be a personal assistant, I figured I could get away with leaving a few shirt buttons undone to show some chest.

I finally drove to the last destination. I entered the coffee shop and was about to order when I realized the cashier was my gym crush. She was 5'6", around my age, half-black with dark green eyes and poofy natural hair. I hadn't seen her in several days, and talking to her excited me.

You don't need to worry about rejection since you have Amanda.

"Hey! You go to the gym down the street, don't you? I'm Mark; I've seen you there a few times." I said pleasantly.

She squinted at me. "Um. Yeah, hey." She pointed to her name tag. It said 'Kiya'.

"Did you change your hair? It looks really nice."

"Oh." She looked surprised. "Well, my friends said I have to stop straightening it and let it go back to being natural; otherwise, it'll get damaged. I'm not sure I like it, though."

I shrugged. "Your friends seem smart; it really suits you."

She looked down, probably trying to figure out if I was being genuine or not. "Are you ready to order?"

"Right! Sorry." I pulled a piece of paper from my breast pocket, unfolded it, and slid it over the counter.

"They warned me about this order." She chuckled nervously.

"I thought it would be easier to deal with if it were all written down."

She took the paper and started tapping on her screen. "It is, actually. So what do you do at this three hundred dollar coffee order company?" She looked me up and down.

Gonna brag or be honest?

"Certified office bitch." I grinned. "I don't actually know what this company even does." I laughed.

She giggled. "Most guys would say they're the CEO or something."

I smiled. "I'm patiently waiting for my promotion." I joked. "Are you gonna hit the gym tonight?"

She looked at me crazy. "It's Friday night! My friends and I are going to the club." She finished with the order and took my card.

"If you change your mind, I'll be there." I took the receipt she'd just printed off. "Thank you—"

Is it K-I-ya, or K-ee-ya?

"K-I-ya." I said confidently.

She beamed at me. "You pronounced it right."

I smiled, left a generous tip on the receipt, and instead of signing, I wrote, 'The gym is way more fun than the club. Promise.'

I said goodbye, took the coffee, and left. Soon, I made it to the office and passed out everyone's coffee. I received several compliments from the men about my new look and many lingering stares from the women. Once I finished handing them out, I made my way to Amanda's office. Gordon wasn't at his desk, so I knocked and entered.

Amanda was sitting at her desk, talking on the phone. She watched me enter and gazed at me. Then, she told the person on the phone that she would have to call them back later. I turned around and clicked the door lock as she hung up.

"Ma'am, I—" I stammered.

She waited, twirling her fingers in her hair. She looked me up and down like I was a menu, deciding what she wanted to eat.

"I'd like to repay you for yesterday, Ma'am," I said purposefully.

Her face lit up. Clearly, that pleased her. She slowly stood and rearranged her desk so it was clear. She quietly stepped around her desk, and I realized she was barefoot again and wearing the same tight black dress she had worn during our interview. She walked gingerly to the front of the desk and deftly pushed herself up to sit on it, her legs dangling off.

She gestured down and whispered, "Partake."

I swallowed and nodded. I was fully erect in seconds from the mere sight of her like this.

I strode toward the desk, stopping in front of her. I knelt down on my knees and sat on my heels. She hurriedly shimmied her dress above her hips, and I saw her beautiful thighs were squished from her sitting, making them look even bigger. She had her legs pressed together, and I could see skimpy black lace panties clinging to her hips. I started at her knees; my hands traveled up the side of her thighs and hooked her panties, slowly pulling them down as she lifted herself slightly. I pulled them all the way down past her ankles and let them fall.

When I saw her feet, I cupped her heel and brought her toes to my mouth without thinking. I swirled my tongue between her toes as she gasped in surprise.

Not right now. Eat.

I regained my composure and pulled her foot away. I lifted her feet, spread her legs, and draped them over my shoulders. I stared at her pussy. It was pretty and pink and beginning to get wet. Her clit was enormous and swollen, and above, she had closely trimmed brown hair.

I lunged at her clit, enveloping it with my mouth and sucking with my tongue, my nose jamming into her abdomen. She squealed in delight. She reached down and ran her fingers through my hair, putting gentle pressure on my head when needed. Her legs trapped my head, and I could faintly hear her talking through her thigh pillows.

"You are SUCH a good boy!" She cried. "Do you love Mommy's pussy?"

I nodded. She tasted like forbidden divinity, the Apple in the Garden.

"Oh my god, I'm getting so wet, but you just keep drinking it!" She said excitedly. "Yes baby, fuck me with your face, you fucking slut!" She moaned, gripping my hair and grinding her pussy into my face. "You're making me cum. You're gonna make Mommy cum!" She said with a gasp and then went silent. Her thighs squeezed tight against my ears. After thirty seconds, her thighs relaxed, and she started breathing raggedly.

"Oh, baby." She cooed. "My sweet baby boy. You made Mommy cum with just your tongue." She was twirling her fingers in my hair. "I knew you were cute when I saw you, but I didn't know you'd make such a good little boy."

Her thighs released my head, and she was allowing me to pull away. I angled my head up and looked into her eyes.

"Please let me make you cum again, Mommy," I whispered against her pussy.

She shuddered, and I dove into her, extending my tongue as far as I could. I licked down to the very bottom of her pussy, nearly reaching her ass, and traveled up, plunging my tongue as deep as I could into her hole. I receded and then savagely attacked her clit.

"Oh FUCK." She croaked. She doubled over, her head just above mine as she was reeling from the pleasure. "Please, oh fuck, baby, I'm- I'm so sensitive." Her legs began trembling, and I reached my arms around her legs to grab the top of her thighs. I felt and squeezed her perfect thighs and used them as leverage to pull my face closer into her.

I was Atlas. She was the Universe.

I sucked and licked and nibbled and bit her clit, experimenting with everything I knew how to do. Making her cum was now the center of my being. I was desperately hungry, devouring her sex as though making her cum was paramount to my survival.

I was starving. She was my food.

I relentlessly pleasured her. Amanda could no longer speak filthy to me any longer; she had devolved into weak little cries and moans. Then, I began feeling a small trickle of liquid below my bottom lip, going down my chin.

"Ohhh ... Sweetie... I haven't... So long..."

I realized what was happening and quickly opened my mouth wider to receive it. She moaned uncontrollably, shuddered violently, her heels planted into my back, and she clamped her thighs around my head so hard my ears started ringing.

"I'm- I'm—" She nearly screamed. Then, with a low whisper. "I'm squirtinggggg ohhh fuckkk. Drink my squirt, drink Mommy's squirt."

Her cum quickly filled my mouth and I swallowed, greedily. I was drinking her squirt like a lost oasis in the desert.

I was thirsty. She was water.

Her delicious orgasm was soon over, and she returned to normal breaths. She pet my hair and relaxed her thighs, letting me back up for air. She looked down at my face between her legs.

"I think that was the best head I've ever had." She said with a weak smile. "Is your cum ready for me?"

I nodded. My cock was steel and leaking precum, it had been since I started. She motioned for me to stand and slid off the desk. She stood me in front of her, looking into my eyes as she unbuckled and dropped my pants. Then, she kissed me.

She kissed my lips, then licked over all of my face, loving the taste of herself. She grabbed my body and squeezed it against herself, my cock pressing straight up against her stomach. She stood on her toes, grabbed my cock with one hand, and positioned it down. Then, she slid it between her pussy lips and thighs.

I hadn't entered her. I had slid between her thighs and was lubricated by her cum and my saliva. She put one foot behind the other and crossed her legs, squeezing me even tighter. She grabbed my hips and forced me to fuck her thighs.

I slipped between her thighs over and over, moaning with the incomprehensible sensation. She started moving me faster, moving herself in sync while I clinged to her, paralyzed.

I was on the edge, precum dribbling out of my dick when she arched her back, and the tip of my cock slipped past to the other side of her thighs, resting directly below her ass. Her thighs squeezed harder, stretching and pulling it, until I grunted, pulsing out cum over and over. My cum splashed onto the desk behind her, pooling into a puddle of milky white.

Slowly, she released me, both of us leaning on the desk to support our weight. She smiled deeply. "You were fantastic."

I grinned back and shrugged. "You taste amazing." I leaned back and let out a satisfied moan. "That... Thigh thing... That was fucking hot."

She giggled. I pulled my pants up, and she led me to her secret bathroom. It was a typical secret bathroom, I suppose. Fancy as fuck and full of things I couldn't afford. Amanda grabbed two plush washcloths, soaked them in warm water, and we each cleaned ourselves well. After I was done, I buckled my pants and leaned on the counter with one hand.

I stared at her. "Miss Jo—" I stopped. "Amanda. I—"

She put her hand on my chest and nodded. She knew what I needed without me having to speak.

I leaned into her, and our lips met. I pulled her body into me and pushed her against the bathroom counter, lifted her legs, and sat her on top. She wrapped her legs around me, her tongue around my tongue as I explored her ass with my hands. We fed on each other, consuming our affection. I wasn't crying, and I wasn't sad, yet tears flowed freely from my eyes. Our lips were sealed together, and we shared the same breath for a while. I exhaled into her, and she breathed my air, then exhaled back into me. We did this as long as we could until we separated, wet, gasping for oxygen.

She caressed my face, memorizing my features. "I've waited for you. For so long —" she brought her fingers, soaked with my tears, to her lips.

I nodded. "I feel like... I'm not as empty anymore."

She smiled. She gently pushed me back, hopped off the counter, and fixed her dress. I followed her as she walked back into her office. She bent over, in a blatant display, and picked up her panties from the floor. She used them to clean my cum off her desk, and I watched as she licked the cum off of them.

She put her cleaned panties back on and winked at me. "Now, we actually do have work to do."

Following our insane pseudo-coitus, the remainder of the day was filled with unyielding paperwork and bureaucracy. Spreadsheet after spreadsheet, powerpoint after powerpoint, we dredged through documentation like Sisyphus and his beloved boulder. Reprieve came at lunchtime. Amanda had an oversized couch placed on the wall opposite the coffee table. She laid across it on her stomach, and I sat at the other end, massaging her feet.

"You're like a Queen, and I'm like a peasant living a fairytale." I said wistfully.

She giggled. "We'll make a Prince of you yet."

Our break ended too soon, and we were back to business. More and more monotony was alleviated only by coffee and flirtatious remarks.

It was an eternal suffering, but we suffered together. After some time, I checked my phone. Realizing it was almost eight at night, I rubbed my sore eyes.

"Do you have plans tonight?" Amanda yawned.

"I was going to hit chest," I said.

"Go then, sweetie." She smiled.

"Are you sure? I can stay if you need me to."

"Baby, you basically took half a Master's degree in one day. Go get strong. I like you strong." She pressed.

"Okay." I nodded. I stood up and stretched, then went to kiss her. "Have a good weekend, Mommy."

As I walked out of her office, she yelled after me. "Monday is the second half!"

I drove home, relaxed with YouTube, and ate a small meal. Then, I picked my favorite gym outfit: an oversized T-shirt and undersized shorts. It made my upper body look big and showed off my legs. I mixed up my pre-workout and drank it as I drove to the gym.

I arrived when it was getting dark outside, and the parking lot was empty. I scanned my barcode, and the glass door to the gym unlocked. I liked going in the middle of the night every once in a while. If I wanted to hit a personal record, no one would be around. The gym was empty and serene, as I expected. I sauntered over to the cable machines and started my warmup.

Once I forced some blood into my chest, I felt ready to lift. I went to the flat bench area and set a good starting weight. Finishing a few sets easily, I stepped it up. I managed four repetitions of my maximum weight.

Feeling fantastic, I added ten pounds to the total. Incredibly, I squeezed out two decent reps, blowing past my personal best. I was feeling a little frisky and decided to risk adding ten more pounds.

Under the weight, I knew it wasn't going well when I couldn't slow the bar's descent as much as I wanted to. I let it sit on my chest for a second, then forced it upward. I only got halfway up before my screaming muscles began to fail, and the weight settled back on my chest. I had to give considerable effort just to keep pressure off my lungs. The struggle bus was parked at the gym, and I was on it.

If you can coordinate pushing with your chest, pulling with your lats, and a massive sit-up, you can probably throw the weight to your hips.

I began breathing fast and deep, trying to oxygenate myself in preparation. Then, I heard a beep from outside. The door opened, a gym bag hit the floor, and someone ran towards me.

Kiya leapt onto the bench and straddled my abdomen. Her feet were planted on the floor, and she grabbed the bar, violently trying to pull it up.

"Push! Push!!" She pleaded.

I exploded my arms upward, forcing the bar to slowly move towards the top. I locked my elbows at the top, and Kiya shoved the bar back into the rack. I finally let go of the weight, which thudded into position, surprising Kiya so much that she lost her footing.

She fell, dropping her ass directly onto my dick. I grunted with the sudden weight, and she threw her arms down to steady herself on my chest. I looked at her in surprise, and she stared at me, embarrassed. She quickly stood up, swung her leg over, and turned around.

"Are you okay?" She squeaked.

"Yes." I coughed. "I am now, thanks to you." I reached down and adjusted myself; her sitting on my lap had redirected some blood flow. I sat up, taking a breather after the ordeal. "That." I chuckled. "That was too much weight."

"You think?" She turned around and giggled at me.

I stood up and started pulling weights off the bar, putting them back on weight racks. Kiya helped me, but she struggled with the forty-five-pound plates, so I took those, and she took the smaller ones. As we put the plates away, I stole glances at her. She was wearing a slightly oversized black t-shirt tucked into green workout shorts that stopped just underneath her ass cheeks, lifting and accentuating, making a perfect heart shape. I had to keep myself from staring. The shade of green perfectly complemented her skin tone. Her ass was like the sun during the eclipse; I couldn't look, but I couldn't look away.

Soon, we were done, and I asked what she was working out today.

"Glutes and hamstrings!" She said proudly.

I couldn't help but grin.

Of course. This is gonna be hard. YOU'RE gonna be hard.

"I haven't done legs since last week, so I'll work out with you."

She looked very pleased with my answer. We started out doing stretches, and I quickly realized just how inflexible I really was. Most stretches we did she did them effortlessly. Doing them together, right next to each other on the floor, often placed me in such a position to stare directly at her ass. I couldn't complain even if I wanted to.

After stretching, we started with deadlifts. A few good sets later, we moved on to barbell RDLs.

"I never feel these in my hamstrings." She complained. "Only in my lower back." She finished her first set.

"Hmm." I was thinking of another hamstring-dominant exercise we could do that would refocus her. I shrugged. "We could try doing them on cables."

I set up a cable machine nearby and demonstrated a cable RDL for her. She watched closely. "Remember, this is a hip hinge, so push your ass back on the way down, stretching your hamstrings. Then squeeze and push your hips forward to come back up." I said.

"Yes, Sir." She said seriously.

My cock began to grow rapidly, hearing her call me Sir.

Both sides of the coin, eh?

My shorts were already super tight since I had a leg pump, which made my half erection feel extremely visible. I glanced at her face, and she met my eyes. I looked away quickly. I couldn't tell if she had noticed or not.

Kiya began mimicking my actions, and I could tell she immediately felt the difference. She slowly bent over, her legs shaking slightly. "Oh my god," she moaned. "I can feel it."

Jesus Christ.

I was standing in front of her at an angle, and I could see her ass in the mirror behind her. She paused at the bottom of the rep, and I gazed at the back of her legs. I saw her tight calves, and above them, her hamstrings were set in a V, cords of muscle pathing their way up to the bottom of her ass. I imagined palming the side of her thighs, pressing my thumbs into the bottom of the V... Squeezing up the muscle, her ass inches from my face... Leaning forward—

Slow your roll. Don't be a creep.

My eyes snapped to her face, and she met my glance. I looked away again quickly. She had seen me staring this time. She grunted as she stood back up, completing the rep.

"I felt that for sure." She said, pausing to take a breath. "I need to do these more often."

She finished her set, and we completed a few more silently. I was about to suggest a new exercise when she spoke.

"Hey, so, since you're here. Do you think you can spot me so I can do a heavy squat?" She asked, looking up at me.

"Of course!" I said, relieved she broke the silence first.

She moved toward a squat rack, set the bar up to her height, and put on a warm-up weight. She completed several reps and then went to add more weight. I saw how much she was putting on and helped her load the other side of the bar. She looked at me for confirmation, and I moved to stand behind her, ready to spot.

Before starting, she pulled off her T-shirt and wore a matching green sports bra. In the mirror, I could see her breasts. They were small and perky, and either she was cold or had piercings.

Jesus fucking Christ.

Her eyes met mine in the mirror, and I quickly snapped my focus down to the floor. When I looked up, she seemed annoyed for some reason. I refocused and squatted down a bit, ready to help if she needed me. She set her face and lifted the bar off the rack.

She started off amazing, doing two complete reps. Her third rep moved to the floor too rapidly, and she struggled to get off the bottom. Thankfully, I didn't need to grab her to help her up since the weight was manageable. I only had to get a little closer and pull up on the bar. I helped her rack the bar, and she slipped while doing so, shoving her ass back into my crotch.

I was still aroused from earlier, and I knew she had felt it.

It was an accident; don't get any ideas.

I moved my hips back so her ass wasn't touching me anymore. I saw her face in the mirror, and she looked embarrassed.

"That might've been too much." She said sheepishly.

I chuckled. I went to both sides of the bar and removed some smaller plates. She completed the rest of her sets without issue.

After we were done, she suggested we finish the workout on the Stairmaster. I hated cardio, but I agreed since she asked. We started the climb, and she made it look effortless. Her cardio was fantastic.

She must play sports.

However, I started pouring sweat within the first minute. After five minutes, my legs and lungs were on fire, and I had to stop.

"I need..." I choked out. "I'm gonna grab some water and hit the bathroom." I climbed down from the machine.

"Big strong man can't climb some stairs?" She giggled. Her laugh was piercingly adorable.

I laughed and moved towards the water fountain. Upon filling my shaker bottle, I desperately gulped down all the contents and had to refill it before using the restroom. I sat at the urinal for much longer than I should've. It was difficult to pee, since my mind would drift off thinking about Kiya, my cock would get hard, and my pee would stop.

After I forced myself to focus and finish, I washed my hands well and left the bathroom.

Kiya was standing next to the water fountain, rubbing her eyes. "What's wrong?" I said, concerned.

She looked up at me; her eyes held sadness and fear. She hadn't been crying, but her eyes were red.

"After today." She whispered. I could barely hear her. "Are you going to go back to ignoring me?"

Huh?

"What are you talking about? I don't—" I replied, bewildered.

"You barely look at me for more than a second. You don't even acknowledge my existence." She said. Her eyes were welling with tears. "I bet you don't even realize we went to fucking high school together."

Wait, is that why she always seemed familiar?

"You were always wrapped up with that prissy-ass bitch," Her Southern Black accent began to emerge, "Who thought she was better than everyone else cause she got into nursing school."

Accurate.

"But... I didn't know—" I stammered.

"Why do you think I even joined this fucking gym?!" She snarled. She was getting angry. "I've been staring at you for fucking YEARS!" Now she was mad.

"Then today, I blew off my friends, I dressed slutty as fuck, I saved your ass on the bench. I fucking pushed up on you—" She got quiet. "You still won't make a move. Am I just fucking disgusting to you?" She whispered, her voice cracking.

I stared down at her. Her face was immaculately tortured, tears flowing across her features. Her eyes were drowning in a sea of longing and pain, one that I knew all too well.

Do or die.

She sneered at me. "Do I have to fucking beg you, SIR—"

I raised my hand, took her by the throat, and shoved her against the wall with a thud. I pressed my body against hers and forced my lips against hers. She melted into me, moaning into my mouth. I danced with her tongue, playing with it behind her teeth. Then I broke the kiss. I pulled away and gently grabbed her hair with my other hand, pulling her head backwards. Her eyes were closed, tears still flowing, but she wore a smile as she breathed raggedly from her open mouth.

I whispered into her ear. "You're the first person I look for when I arrive and the last one I look for when I leave."

She huffed. She either liked what I said or didn't believe me. I let go of her hair and throat, then bent down, grabbed her ass with both hands and lifted. I picked her up easily and slammed her back into the wall. She yelped, then smacked her mouth into mine, biting my lip. I pulled her ass into me, grinding my dick into her. She whimpered, kissing me, then dug her nails into my back. She was feral, ripping at my skin with razors. I loved it. The fact that she had to cause me pain from being in so much pleasure made me want to cum right then. I was getting close. We weren't even naked, but I could feel her pussy lips with only a few layers of thin fabric between us.

She slowed her kissing and scratching, then broke free from my mouth and gasped for breath. "Wait." She whimpered.

Stop. Put her down.

I'd gone too far. I set her down gently, uncupped my hands from her butt, and backed away. I pushed against the wall and released my weight against her.

"Fuck. I'm sorry. I—" I said.

"No, it's okay..." She interjected. She was blushing and wringing her hands.

You dumb, stupid idiot.

I froze. "Oh. Are you still..." I asked slowly, extremely concerned.

She looked up at my expression, then laughed, her embarrassment passing. She put her hand on my chest. "Yes, I've had sex before, Mark."

She said, smiling. "With you I just... I think it should be different." She said thoughtfully.

I smiled. "How about we go to the park tomorrow? It's supposed to be really nice outside; there will be lots of people, and we'll be out in public... So there won't be any pressure for." I gestured between us. "This."

Her face lit up like the Fourth of July in Texas. "That would be so much fun."

She grabbed her gym bag. I opened the door for her and walked her to her car. I put my number in her phone and watched her drive off. I sat in my car, thinking about what had happened. After a few minutes, my phone buzzed, breaking me out of my daydream. It was a text from an unknown number.

Did she change her mind?

I opened my phone and opened the message. It was a picture, an address, and a text.

Amanda.

She had taken a selfie by lowering her phone beneath and behind her. Her black bangs framed her eyes as she peeked over her shoulder at the phone. She had a pure white nightgown draped over her plump ass, and between her cheeks I could see a hint of a white thong.

The text read 'Do you need Mommy?'

I replied 'Fuck yes, I need you.'

I copied the address into Maps and started speeding towards my boss's house.

Chapter Three

Amanda's house was only a short drive across town. She lived in a middle-class neighborhood, and I was surprised that her house was only one story and very modest. The style was limewash brick with black-stained wood accents. She had a sparkling, diamond-black SUV parked in the driveway; I couldn't figure out what it was, but I knew it was expensive. I parked my car on the street, turned it off, and sat thinking, feeling out of place.

You don't deserve her.

I unbuckled the seatbelt, climbed out of the car, and stepped onto the walkway leading to her front door. It was a deep ebony carved with swirls and patterns that only a master could have accomplished. The windows framing the door had curtains drawn, and light trickled through. I slowly walked the path, climbing the mountain of my own fear and insecurity. I stopped short of the porch, staring at the small step.

She deserves everything you are capable of giving.

The door opened, and I looked up. Light flooded onto me, and her image was a prophesied vision. She stood barefoot in her pure white nightgown, ethereally bathed in glow. The slip draped just past her hips, formed up against her waist, and spilled her breasts out the top. Her brown eyes were framed by her black hair and conveyed warm desire. She emanated beauty, an angel trapped within a mortal form.

"Be a good boy and take me already." She whispered.

Be not afraid, for behold...

I rose up the porch before her. She stood in the doorway above me, peering down at my face. I wrapped my arms around her thighs, lifted her up, and walked into the house as she cupped my face in her hands and kissed me.

I set her down in the foyer, reached behind me, and threw the door closed. It collided with the frame and latched while I feasted on her lips. My hands roamed her, trailing across her skin. I needed every single inch of her body. I broke the kiss and ravished her neck, then plunged my face into her cleavage. Her head fell back, and she gasped; her fingers found my hair and caressed my head. My fingers found her hips, and I leaned back to peel up her shiny white gown, revealing a sight I had been aching in my soul to witness.

As I pulled it off her head, I saw her in white lace panties, matching her white lace bra I had glimpsed the day prior. Her breasts tested the bra's structural integrity. A large black floral pattern was tattooed beneath her breasts, contrasting her creamy skin. I adored it briefly, then my gaze fell to her stomach and hips. She had small rolls and stretch marks, lighting across her skin. She was flawed in no way that mattered.

"Take off your shoes." She whispered.

I used my feet to kick them off, and she started pulling my shirt over my head. She flung it to the side, then caressed my shoulders, palmed my chest, then slid her hands down my abdomen. My stomach spasmed at her touch, and my cock strained against the fabric of my shorts painfully. She moved her hands down my waist and frantically pushed them down, releasing me and letting the shorts fall to the floor. She tenderly wrapped her hand around my girth, barely able to touch her fingers and her thumb. She admired it for a second, then looked up to my eyes.

"Make love to me. Right here." She demanded. "I won't wait any longer."

She hurriedly caught her panties with both thumbs and peeled them down her legs. She grabbed my hands, and I supported her as she sat on the hardwood. Then, she pulled me down and laid back. I fell between her legs, crushing myself against her, and coupled my mouth with hers. My chest compressed her breasts, my hands supported her head against the floor, and her hands pulled my waist into her. My cock rested against her pussy. She was dripping wet, and I effortlessly slid my shaft up and down her slit, slipping and searching. I quickly found her entrance and began pushing inside of her. She gasped into my mouth as I started stretching her walls.

I broke the kiss and bent my head down towards her chest. "Oh fuck." I whimpered. The sensation of just the tip inside of her was so intense that my body perceived it as physical pain. I was doubled over, and my face fell, resting between her breasts.

Amanda's arms wrapped around my head instantly, pressing my face deeper into her motherly embrace. She wrapped her legs around my hips, forcing me beyond her entrance with a slow pressure as she moaned in amazement. My mind was shredded into atoms, pulverized by the pleasure I was not equipped to comprehend. I began groaning uncontrollably into her, my mouth open and drooling as I yelled. She pulled me inside herself deeper and deeper with every second.

"You need to fill Mommy up," she whispered urgently. "You will fuck me later. You need to cum inside your Mother. Right now."

Our hips met, and I was entirely inside her, finally complete. She threw her head back and screamed as she came, her orgasm coursing through her body. Her walls tightened around my cock, somehow pulling me even deeper within, extracting my cum. I was exploding, forcing my cum inside of her. My cock had spurted only three times before she was full, and I kept ejaculating over and over. I felt my cum deluge out of her pussy, past my cock, overflowing out onto the floor.

.
.
.
.

Where am I?

.
.

Amanda!

'... out in to the world,
.. don't like what I see,
You could .. Paradise,
But ... like Hell to me.'

I heard singing. It was soft, high pitched, barely a whisper. It was beautiful and terrible. It was a razor slicing through skin and aloe soothing a wound. I felt tears on my face. I felt fingers running through my hair.

'Lying, in between the memories, choking me, and I don't know which way to go, but I'm okay to never know.'

'I don't know which way to go,
but I'm okay to never—'

The angel's voice broke abruptly, and she wept.

AMANDA.

My eyes opened. It was pitch black. My head snapped up from her chest. I pushed my hands against the floor and off of her, looking for her face. She had a hand covering her mouth; she was violently wracked with sobs, her chest dripping with tears.

"Amanda! Oh my god, oh fuck, are you okay?" I said in a panic.

She pulled her hand from her mouth. "No, no, it's okay, I'm okay." She wailed.

She sniffled, trying to clear her nose, and took several deep, exhausted breaths. Quickly, she was able to calm down. She looked at me. Her tears had obliterated her black makeup, causing gorgeous Rorschach patterns around her eyes.

"Are you okay?" I asked, worried.

She smiled weakly and laughed faintly. "Yes, baby. I'm more than okay. I'm happy that... I ended up here. With you." She looked at me with intense affection and concern. "Are you okay, Sweetie?"

"Me? What do you mean?"

"Silly boy, you lost consciousness while you came inside me." She said, petting my chest.

I thought for a second and remembered. "Oh. I- Yeah, I—" I shook my head and smiled at her. "I'm sorry, that was just—"

"Don't apologize." She cupped her hands on my cheeks and pulled my face down for a kiss. "I think. Um." She let my face go and pursed her lips. "I think that means we're in love. That doesn't happen to people who aren't in love."

My heart surged with feeling.

No shit Sherlock, you hadn't figured that out yet?

I stared down at her, my mouth open, my face wet, my arms weak, my stomach pained.

"I am so fucking hungry."

She smiled up at me and gripped my arms. "Let's go make some food."

She made the best ham sandwiches I had ever tasted. I knew all ham sandwiches weren't created equal, but I didn't know adding lettuce and tomato changed the whole experience so much. After we ate, she sat on the couch, and I lay with my head in her lap. She played with my hair as I took everything in.

You need to tell her.

"Something happened at the gym today," I said cautiously.

I gave her a recap of what had happened with Kiya. I spared unnecessary details, but I explained everything that went down. Once I was finished, I breathed a sigh of relief and waited for her to speak.

"That is SO fucking hot." She said, giggling.

"You're not. Mad? Or jealous?" I asked, taken aback.

"No. You're a good boy. I take care of you enough that you aren't interested in whores. So if you are interested, that means there's something real between you." She explained.

I was silent for a time. "I think there is. But how can I—"

AMANDA'S MARK

"Be into two people? It's really not as crazy as you think." I looked up at her face. "I'm your Mommy, but you." She was beaming down at me. "You are also a Daddy!"

Yeah, that tracks.

I blushed and looked away. It made sense. Amanda was giving me something I needed, and I could provide Kiya with something she needed.

"I have to tell her about us," I said decidedly.

"Yes. If she's okay with it, then that's perfect. If not, it wasn't meant to be." She brushed a lock of hair from my face. "That's okay, too." She said softly.

We spoke and held each other. She told me aspects and history of her life, and I reciprocated. She was divorced with no kids, had a master's degree, and had worked for the company for fifteen years. I told her about my abusive parental relationships, my spiral with drug use, self-harm, and recovery. It was amazing to learn about each other. Then, I remembered something I was curious about.

"What does the company even do?"

"We don't *do* anything." She said, laughing.

"What does *that* mean?" I asked.

"The company is an intermediary between third parties and judicial agencies during questionably legal business acquisitions."

"What does THAT mean?" I was so confused.

"Say you have a company that does or makes something specific, and they want to buy a smaller company that does or makes something similar. Both companies must hire lawyers to ensure that neither party gets the short end of the stick. The government has laws, but more importantly, they want a cut. Taxes, fees, fines, whatever you want to call it, the government always gets its money. The lawyers are busy dealing with each other and don't want to do even more work, so they hire us to deal with the government."

"That sounds so complicated and very boring."

"Why do you think I hired you, baby boy?" She teased.

"I don't remember half of what you taught me today," I confessed.

"You don't need to." She shrugged. "It will either come to you when you need it, or you'll improvise on the spot."

I told her about my date with Kiya the following day, and she suggested we go to sleep and not have sex again. That way, I would be fresh for Kiya. I agreed, reluctantly. I grew up religious, but making love with Amanda was the closest I had ever been to God.

We slept in her bed, an Alaskan King, which is a thing, apparently. It was massive, pillowy, and soft. We slept with her breasts against my back and her arms around me, safe.

In the morning, we took a shower together. I did quick work cleaning myself, then took my time cleaning Amanda. First, I washed her hair. With my erection pressed against her ass, it was an extremely pleasurable experience for both of us. I rinsed her hair, then used a washcloth to clean her neck, down her shoulders and arms, then back up to her breasts. Her chest received most of my attention. I spent a long time working up a lather, kneading them as she grinded her ass against me and moaning. I played with her nipples, taking advantage of the plush washcloth to tweak and pull on them, making her squirm and squeeze her thighs together. Once I had my fill, I washed her stomach and thighs, then I kneeled on the floor of the shower and washed her legs and feet. After I was satisfied, I stood and faced her, kissing her while soaping up her ass.

"You are trying to get some." She said finally, breathless.

"Can't blame me for trying," I said, grinning.

"You have your date with Kiya, remember?" She said, then kissed me on the nose.

I pouted at her jokingly. "At least let me make you cum Mommy."

She acted shocked, but she couldn't hide her smile. She put her hand on my chest and kissed me deeply. After she pulled away, she bent over, pointing her ass towards me and put her hands on the shower tile to support herself.

Her black hair slicked down to her shoulders, and water flowed like rivers down her arched back, falling over her heart shaped ass. Her pussy lips peeked out from her cheeks, and between them her hole tempted me. It took absolutely every single ounce of willpower in my soul to keep myself from running my cock through her like a godforsaken fucking animal.

Instead, I slipped my thumb between her lips and massaged her entrance, willing it to open. She moaned as her pussy greedily accepted it, and I slid my thumb deep inside her, searching for her g-spot and applying pressure. I used my middle and ring finger underneath to find her clit, rubbing circles with the fresh supply of pussy juice she rewarded me with. With my other hand, I pulled her ass apart to see her pink wrinkled hole.

"I want you to cum for me Mommy," I begged her. "I need it. Please."

She groaned gutterally in reply, as her legs quivered. I took a breath, leaned down and licked her asshole. She squealed in surprise. I applied pressure, more and more, as she began to relax. Then without warning, I folded my tongue into a point and forced it into her ass, plunging it as far as I could.

"OH FUCK." She yelled. She slammed her ass back hard into my face. "FUCK- FUCK MOMMYS ASS WITH YOUR TONGUE BABY- ohhhhh fu-u-u-u-u-ck." Her voice undulated as an orgasm tore through her body, and she screamed in pleasure at the very end. Her legs were shaking intensely, and when I removed my tongue, her knees gave out. For a split second I had to support her weight with only the hand in her pussy, pulling up between her legs. Quickly, I wrapped my other arm around her body, slid my hand out from under her, and pulled her into an embrace. I rested my head on her shoulder as she convulsed against me.

"Thank you, Mommy. I love making you cum." I whispered in her ear.

"You—" She was breathing ragged, her words pained and desperate. "You are such. A good. Fucking. Boy."

After our shower, I found my old clothes strewn haphazardly in the foyer and put them on. She had draped a black velvet robe around herself.

How is she even sexier in black?

Amanda followed me out the front door, and I stopped, seeing her SUV in the sunlight. It was a brand new Cadillac Escalade. I stopped, my mouth hanging open.

"That thing is a beast," I said.

"I had it supercharged, too." She giggled. I stared at her in disbelief. She mocked embarrassment, smiling. "What? I like going fast."

I looked at my car behind it in comparison. It was a '90s Chevy sedan, clean with little damage but very behind on maintenance. The model had once been a proud contender in NASCAR decades prior, but its glory days were long gone. She walked me to my car. I unlocked it with the key, then climbed into the seat. I was instantly hit with the blistering heat that had festered in the cabin and was embarrassed for what Amanda was about to witness.

I closed the door. On the inside, the manual window crank handle had broken years ago, and the plastic understandably has not survived the past thirty years. I placed my palms flat against the window, forced the mechanism to yield, and slid the window down. I grinned at her sheepishly, mortified.

She bent over and kissed me through the open window. "Drive safe." She gave me a knowing look, having contemplated something. "Have fun on your date, Sweetie." She said, genuinely.

"I'll try," I replied. "I will."

I made my way across town towards my apartment. When I arrived, I snatched a protein yogurt from the fridge to eat, then prepared the best outfit I could currently afford. I put on a pair of simple black shorts that came just above the knee and a crisp white t-shirt with nice thin fabric that showed off my muscles.

I texted Kiya. 'Hey, are you ready for the park?'
She replied almost instantly. 'Of course, let's go!'
I smiled.
No waiting around with this one.
When I got to the park, I sat in the lot for a few minutes, texting her where I was and what my car looked like. Soon after, a white Ford SUV with tinted windows pulled up beside me. Kiya turned off the car, hopped out, and ran to where I stood.

"Hi Mark!" She said excitedly, giving me a quick hug.

Somehow, we had read each other's minds. She was wearing a white V-neck T-shirt that displayed her small cleavage and tight black gym shorts. My eyes traveled down her muscular legs and stopped at her feet.

Good Lord.

She was wearing white flip-flops that contrasted the color of her melanin skin. Her toes were painted the same shade of green as her gym outfit the day before.

"Your nails are so fucking adorable." I blurted.

"Thank you!" she said proudly. "I can't believe we're matching. You must like me, " she said in a singsong voice.

I laughed, grabbed her hand, and led her into the park.

We strolled through the park, talking, laughing, and enjoying each other's company. I physically could not keep my hands off of her. My hands were either clasped with hers, grabbing her waist, or copping quick feels of her ass. I took every advantage possible of finally being able to touch her, and she leaned into me every time, obviously content with my obsession over her.

After a few hours, we lounged on the shallow slope of a grassy hill, staring at the clouds.

"Let me massage your feet," I said, suddenly.

"Why?" She stated, looking sideways at me. "Oh my god, are you into feet?" She asked, giggling.

"Yeah, it's a new development." I shrugged. "I mean, if we weren't in public I'd suck your toes, but we can't do that here, can we?" I teased.

"Okay, I guess, but don't do too much because I'm ticklish."

I crawled in front of her and sat cross-legged. I pulled her sandals off, then put her feet in my lap. I focused on one at a time, finding that she held knots in her arches. I was slow and deliberate, using the strength in my thumbs to grind away the tension. We were both enjoying it immensely. My cock was swollen and beginning to make itself known, and she was faintly moaning as I relived the pressure in her feet.

"What sport do you play?" I asked.

"Basketball, " she replied. She lay back in the sun, her eyes closed, her face serene, as I serviced her. "My friends and I are on the college team," she said.

"That's cool. I never got too into sports. I wrestled for a few years but didn't stick with it. Plus, remember the popular Black guy in our class? The couch always matched us together and I always got my shit pushed in by him."

"He was a total fucking bully." She said. Clearly, she didn't have fond memories of him either. "Is that why you suddenly became the class clown? So, he'd stop bullying you as much? If you had just stood up to him, I think he would've stopped."

"You're probably right." I sighed. "But my dad said he'd punish me if I got into a fight, even to defend myself, so... Being funny kind of eased me off his radar."

"Well, I always thought cute and funny was a good combo for you." She said wistfully.

I smiled. If only I had been with her in high school instead of my ex, I could've saved myself so much heartache.

Now is as good a time as any.

"Listen, Kiya. I like you a lot and don't want to hide anything from you." I said, awkwardly. "I'm seeing another woman, and I like her too—"

"I have a roster too, y'know." She snapped. She had tried to sound playful, but I could hear the sharpness in her tone.

I shrugged. "You *are* fine as fuck."

She sighed and sat up. "I get it; I'm not expecting us to be exclusive right away. We're only in the talking stage or whatever."

I nodded. "I know. I just prefer being upfront and honest. Well, actually, I just hate lying. Trying to keep up a lie is so exhausting. Too much dumb shit to remember. It's easier being honest all the time." I said, letting her feet rest in my lap.

"Honesty is a good quality." She said thoughtfully. Then, she gave me a stare I could only describe as competitive. "I think you might have other good..." She started rubbing her feet against my cock, teasing me. "Qualities... as well."

I grinned at her, suddenly emboldened. "Are you *trying* to get fucked?" I teased her back.

Risky.

"Not here." She said with a mischievous grin.

She yanked her feet out of my lap, snatched up her sandals, stood up, and took off running barefoot through the grass.

Where the fuck is she going?

I took off after her, considerably slower. Cardio was not my forte. When I made it up the hill, I saw her a few hundred yards across the park, at the edge of the parking lot. She looked at me with fire in her eyes. She put on her sandals, then briskly walked towards her vehicle. I hurried to catch up. After a minute or two, I made it to the parking lot just in time to see her open the SUV's back door, where she stood waiting for me. I walked up to her, breathless. I looked around. The parking had become a tight fit, cars packed close to each other. A vehicle was directly beside us, and the door blocked the view from the park. I didn't see anyone around.

"Get in." She whispered.

I climbed into her backseat and sat down. She grabbed my shirt and pulled me flat, my back against the bench seat, my head towards the open door. I angled my chin towards her, watching as she looked around. Without warning, she dropped her shorts, stepped out of them, and threw them past me. She clambered over me, slamming the car door, and sat on my face.

Her pussy was completely shaved and already wet. I plunged my tongue inside of her, relishing the sweaty taste. She desperately shoved my shorts down to my knees and grabbed my rock hard cock with both hands.

"Oh fuck." She whimpered. I didn't know if she was surprised by my pussy-eating, or by my cock, but I didn't care.

I went to town between her legs, eating her like it was my last meal. I felt her warm lips envelope my tip, and I moaned into her. I refocused my mouth onto her clit, swirling my tongue around in patterns. She gasped onto my dick, then bobbed her head up and down, trying to force more of me into her mouth. She only made it about halfway down before she began choking and had to come up for air.

"Oh fuuuuuck, Daddy, that feels so good." She cried, grabbing my cock and gripping the shaft tight. Her hand wrapped around the base of me and left a little over two inches free. She had found her limit, so set her hand and started sloppily devouring what she could of my dick.

Her saliva was flowing down her hand into my lap, while her cream flowed down my cheeks and neck. I was moaning into her pussy, her mouth and tongue causing my cock to spasm and twitch. I must've done something right, because she started yelling, muffled by my dick, her ass quivering and shaking on my face, and soon I was rewarded by a fresh supply of cream leaking into my mouth.

She pulled her head away from my lap and gasped. "Daddy." She whined. "Sit uuuup."

I obliged, and we maneuvered in the tight space so that I was sitting on the bench, with her in my lap. She straddled me with her bare muscled thighs squeezing my hips, her calves folded underneath, and her feet hanging off the bench. My cock stood straight up and her pussy slid against it, lubricated with cream, saliva, and my precum. She ground against me desperately, our foreheads pressed together as we stared down, aching for the act. I was gripping her ass tight, and I lifted her off me slightly, letting my dick drop past her lips, set at the perfect angle aligned at her entrance.

Hold on. Remember?

"Wait," I whispered.

Her face snapped up, and I met her eyes. Her gaze was twisted and crazed with lust. Every ounce of her being wanted to be fucked into oblivion. I gently pushed her hips away from my lap, setting her back down onto my legs. Her face slowly returned to normal, realizing how close we had come.

"Right." She nodded, catching her breath. "Fuck you Mark, god damnit!" She was bouncing on my legs, laughing. She raised her head to the ceiling of the car and moaned. "Oh my gooood, what the fuck are you doing to me."

I was smiling from ear to ear. "That was so fucking sexy. But I know you didn't want to... Y'know."

"Yeah, I know." She bent her head back down and met my eyes. "I am still going to make you cum, though." She stated, matter-of-factly.

She climbed off my lap and made a show of pushing me to the far side of the seat. She sat on her knees and bent over, and took me back into her mouth, slurping and sucking wildly. I threw my head back and groaned.

"Oh fuck. Kiya- Oh my god. Fuck, I—" I dropped my head back down to watch. She was ferocious, attacking my cock like it pissed her off. My orgasm was spooling inside of me, building to the point of no return. I looked over to the side and watched her arched waist and perfect ass. I reached my arm over her back and slid two fingers down between her ass, slipping both effortlessly inside her pussy. She gasped and moaned around my cock. I dug my fingers deeper inside her, using them as leverage to pull her deeper around my dick. She was so fucking hot, and her cries of pleasure reverberated around my dick and sent me over the edge.

"Fuck I'm- Fuck Kiya, you're making Daddy cum!" I released into her, filling her mouth, forcing her to swallow so she could continue accepting my cum. Her pussy squeezed my fingers tight, and she opened her mouth, my dick muffling her scream as cum dropped from her mouth, and cream dripped from my fingers.

She recovered quickly, and lazily cleaned my cock with her tongue, not wanting to waste a drop.

"You are a very Good Girl." I sighed, impressed and spent.

Soon, she lifted herself up, then sat on the seat leaning back, exhausted. She weakly gestured between the both of us. "I need. I need more of this, please. Fuck. That was so hot."

I grinned, my head still reeling from my orgasm. "Anything for you, Darling."

We cleaned ourselves with napkins from her glovebox, put our clothes back on, moved to the front seats, and blasted the AC.

"The windows got so foggy." She giggled, covering her mouth with her hand. "I hope nobody saw."

"If they did, they probably just thought we were hotboxing a blunt or something." I reasoned.

"True." She agreed. "I have a basketball game on Monday; it's a home game. Do you wanna come?"

"Fuck yeah," I said, beaming at her.

We left the park and went our separate ways. I used the remainder of the day for chores at my apartment, then decided to finish out with a good back day at the gym. When it came to my back, I liked to put a special focus on my lats, traps, and rear delts. It brought an extra definition to my muscles and made me look extraordinarily broad-shouldered and wide. When I was satisfied with my work, I went into the bathroom, stripped off my shirt, and flexed my back in the mirror. I held my phone in selfie mode over my shoulder, testing the best angle. After a few minutes, I was finally happy with one of my pictures. My face was in profile above my shoulder, and my ass looked plump in the shorts I was wearing. The main focus was my back, which looked enormous, rippling with snakes of muscle. I cropped it a little, put on a dark filter to bring out more definition, and sent the photo to Amanda and Kiya.

Kiya replied within seconds. 'Are *YOU* trying to get fucked????'

I laughed and grinned from ear to ear. 'Just showing off and rewarding my good girl.' I sent back.

After sending the texts, I threw my shirt back on and left the gym. As I opened my car door, I realized my phone was vibrating. I got in, started it, and closed the door. When I looked at my phone, I saw a missed call from Amanda. I called her back immediately.

"How does it feel to be God's favorite?" She purred, answering the phone.

I laughed. "Well... Thanks, I thought you'd enjoy it."

"How was your date?"

"It was really good, actually."

"Did you cum?"

"I- Uh—" I stammered. "Yeah, I did. But we didn't have sex."

"Then *cum*." She emphasized. "Over... and fuck your Mommy."

"Oh shit. Yes Ma'am. I'm on my way."

I hung up the phone and saw I had multiple messages from Kiya. She had sent me two pictures. The first was of her in front of a long mirror that rested on the floor. She was leaning forward, the back of her legs towards the mirror, with her face upside down. Her arms wrapped around her knees, where she held her phone. Her muscled hamstrings were displayed proudly and atop them her ass was perfectly curved. There was a small gap between her thighs where her lips peaked out. Cream dripped from her pussy down her legs.

Good. FUCKING. God.

I caught my breath and opened the next photo. She was sitting in front of the mirror, frog style. Her phone was in front of her face, her hair displayed around it. Her chest was bare, her perfectly small breasts centered, and her nipples pierced with small silver bars.

I knew it.

Her thick thighs were spread and squished against her calves, with her tiny feet peeking out behind her. I could see her smooth pussy, and something blue between it and the floor.

Is that . ?

I realized she was sat on a dildo, and it was entirely inside her. My phone vibrated with another message from her.

"I'm practicing for you, Daddy." She sent.

"You are *such* a Good Girl." I sent back.

"I'm only good for you, Daddy." She replied.

My face had a permanent smile and my cock was painfully pressed against my shorts. I put my phone down, focused, and started my short trip to Amanda's house.

Chapter Four

I pulled up to Amanda's house and parked the car on the street, concerned.

Who the fuck is here at this time of night?

A sparkling black Corvette was parked in her driveway in front of her SUV. I exited my car, and Amanda threw open the front door and ran to meet me. She was wearing a black two-piece pajama set. She had a massive smile on her face and enveloped me in a big hug.

"What's... going on?" I asked slowly.

Amanda hopped up and down, ecstatic and unable to contain her excitement. "I bought you a new car!" she squealed. And it matches mine!"

There's no fuckin' way.

"You didn't have to... What?" I stuttered. "I mean, I don't need a new car, especially one as expensive as this."

The car was a C7, and it was beautiful. It had aggressive lines and scorching curves, complete with a big wing on the back and a badge on the front that said 'Z06.'

"Yes. You. Do." She tapped me on the chest three times. "You deserve it, baby boy." She gave me an evil grin. "This one is supercharged, too."

I might cum right now.

"Amanda, I- I don't know what to say," I said faintly. "Thank you. So much. It's incredible."

"Oh, just wait." She grinned. "You have to take me on a test drive."

We went the speed limit through town, making our way to the outskirts where there was a long, flat, uninterrupted road. Once I found a perfect spot, I stopped the car, centered on the middle lines. I looked at Amanda.

"Go for it, baby." She whispered, grinning.

First gear. I eased the accelerator, having found out that first gear would break the tires off the pavement easier than I had imagined. I was trying to get up to speed, not do a burnout. Once I hit 25mph, I slammed the pedal down. I had to tap the paddle shifter quickly to avoid redlining.

Second gear. The engine rewarded me with an explosion out of the exhaust, slamming us into our seats as the car propelled forward. The supercharger squealed, screaming as it gulped down air. The rear end of the car swayed, and I had to compensate slightly but was able to regain control. Before I knew it, we had already passed the speed limit.

Third gear. The car had caught its stride. It liked going fast and preferred it. It was glued to the pavement, steadily increasing speed. Its hunger for the road was unyielding. 'Faster,' it urged. 'Faster. FASTER.'

Fourth gear. I took shallow, controlled breaths. Any sudden movement could send us careening off the road. I could feel my heartbeat in my throat. My hands had a film of sweat, making it difficult to hold the steering wheel properly. I was losing it, but I couldn't let go. 126mph. 128mph. 130mph.

Just a little more. Just one more.

I was terrified and exhilarated. I was frozen, and I was free.

131mph.

I let my foot off the accelerator. The engine let out deep rumblings and pops as it immediately slowed down. I took a huge breath in and sighed as it decelerated to 100mph. My fingers were tingling, and my arms were numb. I glanced over at Amanda as we coasted.

She was smiling wildly. "Good job, baby."

I grinned. "I think I'm good for tonight. I don't wanna push my luck." I looked back at the road and let the engine wind itself back down to the speed limit. Soon, I found a turnoff and started making my way back to Amanda's house.

On the drive back, I noticed Amanda squirming in her seat, seeming uncomfortable. "What's wrong?" I asked.

She looked over to me, her face flushed and red. "It's nothing, baby... it's just that... the suspension is so stiff... and it's vibrating my seat so much."

Holy shit, she's getting off just from the bumps in the road.

"Y'know what the good thing about driving an automatic is?" She asked in a low whisper.

"What's that?" I replied, confused.

"You only need one hand to drive."

She grabbed my hand and shoved it between her legs. She was warm and wet, and I could feel her soaking through her silk shorts. I was instantly hard. I quickly pulled my hand back slightly and slid underneath her shorts and found her clit. Her arms were straight, pinning her breasts together as her hands pushed mine down into her crotch. I reached my finger down to her entrance and slid upward, taking advantage of how wet she already was to lubricate her clit. I kept my eyes on the road while I was half leaned over, playing with her pussy.

It only took a minute of my attention for her to cum. Her thighs clamped down on my hand as her body shook, and she whispered, "I'm cuminggggg." She leaned back in the seat, breathless, and I pulled my hand from her lap as I pulled the car into her driveway. I parked and pulled the keys out of the ignition. She grabbed my face, roughly pulling me to her, and kissed me.

"Mommy." She kissed. "Needs to fuck." She kissed. "Her fuck toy." She kissed. "Right. Now." She shoved her tongue down my throat.

I REALLY might cum right now.

She pushed me back into my seat, unbuckled herself, threw open the car door, and deftly got out. I sat in the seat for a second, my mind reeling as I unbuckled. Then, my car door opened. She grabbed me with both hands, yanked me out of the car, and dragged me up to the house. She snatched the keys out of my hand and opened the door. We walked inside, and she slammed the door behind us.

She stood with her hand on her hip and pointed to the back of the house. "Bedroom. NOW." She ordered.

Without a second thought, I sprinted to the room. The door was already open. Got in and figured she wanted me naked. I stripped off my shirt, kicked off my shoes, and ripped down my shorts. I clambered onto the bed, laid flat, and waited patiently. She walked in quickly, saw my clothes and position, then nodded.

"Good Boy."

I swallowed. She unbuttoned her pajama top, threw it off, bent over, and pulled down her shorts. Then, she walked over to the corner of the bed. She reached under the bed and pulled something black out. She snatched my ankle and pulled it towards her, then tied a restraint around it. I swallowed again. She walked to the other three corners of the bed and restrained my other ankle and my wrists, forcing me to lay spread-eagle. She climbed onto the bed and stood over me, her legs outside my hips. With her feet flat on the bed, she squatted down, hovering over my cock that was dripping precum down the shaft. She grabbed it with one hand and rubbed it tenderly against her clit and entrance, then set it gingerly inside. She put her hands on my chest, her arms pressing her breasts together towards my face as she bobbed up and down, my dick barely inside her. She looked at me, waiting.

I whimpered at the feeling, my cock aching to be inside her. I pushed my hips off the bed slightly, trying to get inside of her. She looked at me below her bangs, and fire ignited in her eyes.

"Bad boy." She snarled. She raised one of her hands and slapped me across the face.

Her impact wasn't hard, but it took my breath away and stung my cheek. I let my hips fall back down to the bed. "I'm sorry," I whispered.

She caressed my struck cheek and replied. "Beg."

Submit or suffer.

"Please, Mommy. Please I want—" I pleaded. "I NEED your pussy. Oh fuck I need your pussy, I can't live without it."

She sat deeper by an inch, and her walls clenched down on me. She was dripping pussy juice down my shaft, and it caused my cock to spasm and I pushed, spilling precum inside of her.

"Fuck Mommy please, oh god I can't- I can't- I'm going to fucking die if you don't fuck me." I cried, praying to my goddess.

She slammed her ass down into my lap, enveloping my entire cock in one motion. My back arched, and my eyes saw stars. The universe was aligned through the focal point of us, and I was liberated of my soul until she spoke me back into existence.

"Take a breath, or you're going to pass out." She said firmly.

I gasped, breathing in deeply, fighting the descent into unconsciousness. I raised my head and saw her in all her glory as she sat on my cock. Her knees were pointed away, her breasts a painting of which only a majesty of song could portray. She was the visage of Athena, her battle: my will.

"Oh, Mommy," I whispered. "You're so pretty."

She smiled, then rode me savagely. I was helpless, only able to watch as her cunt slid up and down my cock in rhythm. I was her toy, her plaything. I ascended and worshiped her, her body relinquishing my sins as I was made divine.

Once, twice, three times she came on my dick, quivering and moaning as her orgasm passed, then she resumed fucking me even harder than before. Her breasts were bouncing between her arms, and I raised my head to feel them on my face. She was relentless, and I was nearing the point of no return.

"Fuck Mommy oh my god, I love your pussy, I love you pussy so much it feels so good, oh fuck oh shit, shit shit shit shit" I whimpered. "I'm gonna, I'm gonna- I can't hold it—"

"No."

She stood up on the bed, instantly releasing me from her. I gasped, the sudden absence of her a knife withdrawn from the wound. I wept, my cock pulsing, begging, yearning for the comfort of her salvation.

Amanda stood over me, dripping from her pussy.

"You can cum when you earn it, Sweetie." She said softly.

"Yes, Mommy," I said. I would not disappoint her again. I ached for her, like an acolyte for a God.

"You're welcome, baby. Now, it's your turn to fuck me."

She stepped off the bed and quickly removed all of my restraints. I sat up, rubbing my wrists, still on the verge of orgasm. She laid on her back, her ass at the edge of the bed, and spread her legs. My lust for her intensified.

"Fuck me. Hard. Harder than any bitch you've fucked before." She commanded.

I got off the bed and moved between her thighs. I lathered my dick in her pussy juice and slowly entered her as she moaned. I positioned my arms below her legs, with her bent knees resting on my elbows, and folded her in half. Her arms were down by her ass, so I grabbed her wrists and locked her open. She raised her head, looking at me in surprise. I pulled back and slammed my entire weight and all the force I was capable of generating into her.

"OH FUCK!" She screamed at the top of her lungs. Her voice pierced my eardrums. I felt the tip of my cock hit her cervix.

I fucked her. Hard. I was not moving of my own volition. My body was acting in response to her command. She spoke fractions of words every time my cock smashed her cervix.

"Fu- ck- Mom- my- oh- fu- u- u- u- uck." She cried.

I was using everything in myself to please her, to give her what she needed. I was pulling her wrists towards me harder with every thrust. I was spending the last of myself, for her, and my head fell between her bouncing breasts as I continued fucking her the best I could.

"Please Mommy, please I need you to cum. Cum on my dick. Cum on my dick Mommy. Please Mommy, please I need you to cum, please cum. Make me a good boy, please Mommy CUM!" I pleaded in desperation.

I felt a tremendous pressure against my dick, and I had to thrust even harder to overcome her pussy squeezing me. Then my entire lap began to get wet.

"I'm- I'm- I'm- squi- squi- squirt- t- t- ting—" She moaned.

Every time I pulled away, she shot a jet of squirt into my crotch, and every time I thrusted, the jet pressurized and sprayed against us, showering us in liquid, over and over and over. With my head hung down and my mouth open, I was able to drink when it sprayed into my face. I was soaking in her squirt, and I couldn't hold my cum in any longer.

"Mommy, PLEASE!" I yelled, nearly in tears.

"C- c- c- cu- cu- cum- in- me—" She gasped.

I emptied myself inside of her, slamming into her as hard as I could. It exploded out of her pussy, combined with her squirt, and gushed down the side of the bed. I thrusted several more times, my body forcing the rest of my cum inside of her, my will spent. I released her wrists and collapsed on top of her, moaning incoherently, our slippery warm cum dripping down our legs.

She pet my hair and shook me. "Let's go take a shower, baby." Her voice was frail and content.

I groaned in acceptance. I was drunk and high. I was on a mountain and below the sea. It was the hardest I had ever came, even recently, tenfold beyond the orgasms I had before Amanda. I slowly stood myself up and helped her off the bed. When she stood, her legs were shaking, and I began swaying. She reached and pulled my arm over her, supporting me, and we walked to the bathroom together.

We stepped into the shower, and this time, she cleaned me. She washed my hair, down my arms, my chest, my cock. She cleaned my legs and back, set me against the shower, and washed herself. I gazed at the goddess, soaping herself up, and she enjoyed the attention. Even in my catatonic state, I still lusted after her. She was the world, and I was eternally hers. She finished drying us off, and we stumbled back to her bed.

"I'll clean it later." She whispered. She climbed into bed and laid on her back. "Come here. Lay on Mommy."

I got in after her and laid my head on her chest, my head and neck supported by her billowy breasts. I fell asleep, her fingers in my hair as she whispered to me.

"You're such a good boy. You fucked Mommy so well, baby. You gave me exactly what I needed. I needed you. I needed your cock. I think... I think I—"

I woke up first the next morning and found Amanda lying on the other side of the bed. I had a painful case of morning wood, so I slowly stroked my thick and swollen cock. I stared at her, thinking about the previous night. She shuffled and rolled over onto her back, still sleeping. I crawled under the covers and took the opportunity to pleasure her. I laid my head between her legs, and couldn't help but grind my dick against the mattress as I licked her. She woke up, already cumming, my fingers inside of her, my tongue gently caressing her clit.

"Fuck baby... Your tongue is... Oh fuckkk." She purred sleepily.

Once I had eaten my breakfast, I climbed up next to her. "Good morning, beautiful."

She sleepily put her hand on my cheek, smiling. "Good morning, handsome. Let me return the favor." She licked her lips. "Breakfast."

I laid back on the bed, and she sat up, then spread on all fours and took me in her mouth. She was an expert, and it seemed her throat was bottomless. Her tongue was between my cock and her lower teeth and she slid down until her throat was fucking me. She gulped me up and down, up and down, and I couldn't hold my orgasm any longer. I came down her throat, and she swallowed everything, not wanting to waste. She eased off of me, using her hand to milk me and get every last drop.

We both lay in bed, content. Amanda sat up, remembering something. "So, how did you not have sex with Kiya?"

I looked at her, blushing. "Um, we almost did in the car at the park. But... I stopped before it got too far."

"Did she tell you she wanted to take it slow?"

"Not exactly. She said she wanted it to be 'different'. So, I didn't... Y'know... Cause I figured that's what she wanted."

Amanda gave me a sad smile. She knew something I didn't. "She wants you, baby. Just realize that she is the one waiting for you, not the other way around."

We got out of bed and made breakfast together, eating, talking, laughing, and loving. Just before noon, I realized it was already Sunday.

"I need to get groceries and stuff for the week," I said.

"Go on, Sweetie. Tomorrow is going to be another lesson." She said.

"Are you... Sure? About the car?" I hesitantly asked.

"Yes. The title is in the glovebox, so make sure you put that somewhere safe."

I grinned. "Yes, Ma'am."

She put her hand on my cheek. "When I comes to Kiya. Don't hold yourself back so much. Girls like passion, okay?"

"Okay," I said. "I think I understand."

She kissed me goodbye, and I grabbed the Corvette key and went to start my new car. I took the scenic route home, enjoying the Sunday drive. I stepped into my apartment, changed my clothes, inspected the fridge, made a list, and headed back out.

I had a full shopping cart and was almost done. I pulled out my phone and opened Kiya's messages to ask her to come over for dinner, and I saw her magnificent pictures. Then, I felt hands on my face, and then, darkness. A small woman had covered my eyes and pressed her body against me. I felt small breasts with nipple piercings pressing into my back.

Did I summon a succubus?

"Guess who?" Her voice chimed.

"Either a good girl or a bad girl, I haven't decided yet," I said.

My eyes were released, and I heard multiple women giggling. I turned around and saw Kiya with three girls in basketball uniforms. Two of the girls were Black, one my height and thick, one shorter than all of us and smaller than Kiya. The third was a very tall and lanky Asian girl. The larger Black girl snatched my phone.

"Oh my god K your titties are so cutteeee." She said, gaping at the pictures. She turned around to show the other girls, who were staring and nodding.

Kiya looked up at me, embarrassed, and looked back down at the ground. "That's Shayna. The tall and short ones are Lin and Mindy."

"It's nice to meet you," I said, unashamed and grinning.

Shayna returned my phone with a devious look and shook my hand. The other two smiled at me.

"Why are you looking at tits and ass at the grocery store?" Shayna asked, giggling.

Suddenly, I changed my mind. I had a better idea.

"I was going to ask Kiya to come to the gym with me," I said, looking at her directly.

Kiya looked up at me. "We just had practice... and we have a game tomorrow, so I don't really want to—"

I raised an eyebrow and interrupted her pointedly. "I need a spotter."

"Oh. Okay, yeah, I'll meet you there tonight, then." She said meekly.

"Perfect," I said, pleased. "I need to get going. You ladies have a great game tomorrow." As I walked away, I was able to catch them gabbing quietly.

"He's pretty," said Mindy.

"You didn't say he was built like *that*," said Lin.

"He's not pretty; he's hot. If you don't fuck him, then *I'm*—" said Shayna.

"Shut. Up!" Said Kiya.

I grinned as I walked to the checkout.

Stuffing groceries into the nonexistent storage space of the Corvette didn't work out, so I had to fit everything in the passenger seat. I got back home and put everything away, then completed some chores I had let get away from me. Around 7 pm, I made my way to the gym.

By the time I arrived, Kiya was already inside. Only one other car was in the parking lot, and she watched me get out of the new car.

"When did you get that?" She asked, dumbfounded.

"My boss gave it to me." I shrugged. "It's... kind of like a bonus."

"Jesus. Dick that good, huh?" She joked.

"Fuck around and find out." I teased back, making her blush.

She was fairly quiet during my workout. I focused mainly on my shoulders. She spotted me when I asked, but I never told her I could easily control the weight. I just wanted her there with me. I desperately wanted to touch her—to feel her—but an older man, the owner of the other car in the lot, was walking on the treadmill.

I couldn't keep my eyes off of her. She was wearing red shorts that were somehow smaller than the green pair, and cupped her ass even tighter. Her ass jiggled like water when she walked, but I didn't touch her. I couldn't. Not yet.

She noticed that I wasn't feeling her up, even when she gave me opportunities, such as bending over to pick up weights. I kept my hands to myself. I could see her getting annoyed and frustrated. My plan started unraveling because of the older man, but it wasn't his fault.

After a few more sets, I spied the older man toweling off, then leaving.

Thank God. Let's see if it's not too late.

Kiya had started acting huffy, bratty even. I told her I was moving, and I went to a bench in front of the free weights. I set the bench at 90 degrees and lowered it two notches. I grabbed two heavy dumbbells and sat on the bench, slightly lower than straight up.

"Kiya, be a good girl and spot me, please," I said, after I had lifted the weights to my shoulders.

She eyed me with suspicion, and I could see her mind contemplating whether to be defiant or obey. Finally, she spoke in a low voice. "Okay."

She started walking behind the bench.

"No." I stared at her. She glared back, confused. I pointedly looked at my lap. She looked at my face and my lap a few times, then moved over in front of me, pouting. She climbed into my lap, her face inches from mine, her feet firmly on the floor, her pussy set on my cock.

She raised her hands below my elbows, and I started my set. She watched my muscles moving, my skin sweating, and my veins popping up close. I did four reps with ease, then had to use more effort. Finishing my set, I had to drive through my legs into the floor to lift the weight, slightly compromising my form and lifting out of the seat. For every rep, I grunted loudly and with effort. I moved out of the seat and sat back down as I lowered the weight. Kiya would move up in my lap with me, then bounce back down at the end of the rep, letting out a tiny gasp. Feeling her bounce in my lap and gasp was turning me on, and it became difficult to focus when her gasps got louder, her clit making contact with my hard cock. I finished the set and dropped the weights to the floor, startling Kiya and making her bounce one last time.

I stared at her, inches from her face. I was sweating, full of adrenaline, hard as a rock, and ready to conquer.

"Yes or no," I stated simply.

"What?" she whispered. Her eyelids were drooping, and her mouth was open; she was about to kiss me.

"Yes," I said again. "Or no."

"Yes, but I—"

I kissed her fiercely and stood up, grabbing her ass to support her weight against me. She instinctively wrapped her arms around my neck and legs around my waist. I quickly walked towards the water fountain that was by the locker rooms. I set her down and broke the kiss.

"Wha- uh—" she protested. I grabbed the hair at the base of her neck into a fist and pushed her into the women's locker room.

"Mark, what are you—" she whined. Walking in, I found a fresh cotton towel rack and grabbed one. I let go of her hair, and she looked at me, bewildered. I twisted the towel up tight.

"Open your mouth," I demanded.

She looked confused, curious, and a little frightened but opened almost without hesitation. I placed the towel in her mouth.

"You have to be quiet in case someone walks into the gym," I whispered, my finger over my lips.

She nodded slowly. I pushed her deeper into the locker room, where wooden benches were bolted to the floor.

"Bend over. Put your hands on the bench."

She did what I asked.

Amazing.

I stepped behind her and peeled down her shorts, revealing that she hadn't worn panties.

"You're a bad girl, aren't you?" I said smiling.

She shook her head no. I dropped her shorts down to her ankles, and looked up her muscular legs and tight ass from behind. Her pussy lips peaked between her thigh gap. I quickly wet my middle finger and, without warning, inserted it inside her.

"Jesus Christ," I whispered. "Your pussy is so small. I don't know if I'm gonna fit." I massaged her internally, gently draping over her g spot, pulling my finger out and pushing it back in. She was getting wetter and whimpering behind the towel. I went as deep as I could go, my finger all the way inside her, and curved it, applying pressure, trying to pull it out. Her ass moved backwards towards my hand, and with my other hand, I smacked my open palm on her ass. Hard. It left a large red handprint.

"Bad girl," I spoke, my voice gravel. I didn't recognize it. "Stay still."

She whimpered, then nodded.

I moved my finger in deep, pulled it out, then put it together with my ring finger and spit on them. I began easing both fingers inside her as she moaned.

"Oh shit." I marveled at the tightness of her. "We're not even close yet."

I manipulated both fingers inside her, maneuvering around her vaginal walls, working her open. When I was satisfied, I pulled them out and combined my ring, middle, and pointer fingers together. I dragged them up and down her slit, then put pressure at her entrance.

She immediately began squealing through the towel.

"Shh," I whispered. "Relax."

She relaxed slightly, and slowly I pushed my fingers into her. I spit on them several times, and after a few moments of pushing in, pulling back, and pushing in, I was stopped at the middle knuckles of my fingers.

I moved my thumb downwards, and thankfully was able to reach her clit. It was wet, and I rubbed it gently before squeezing it hard towards my other fingers. Her ass clenched around my hand, and all three fingers slid into her to the base of my hand as she bit into the towel and screamed.

I rubbed her clit with my thumb, and pressed with all fingers into her g spot, and her legs began quivering.

"Now this," I said, my voice low. "This is almost my size."

Her head snapped backwards, and she looked at me, incredulous. I nodded and worked my fingers inside of her. Within seconds I found her rhythm and she began cumming, moaning into the towel, and creaming all over my fingers. After she had recovered, her legs shaking, I slowly pulled my fingers out of her. I stood her up, pulled her standing, pulled the towel away, and shoved my fingers into her mouth. She eagerly devoured her cum, then looked at me with puppy dog eyes.

"Did I do good Daddy?" She asked cutely.

"Yes, you did," I replied. "Now I'll ask again: yes or no?"

"Yes." She said, hesitantly. "But what—"

"I'm done," I stated. "I'm done waiting. If you're quiet, we won't have to use the towel."

Her eyes widened, and her thighs squeezed together in anticipation. I pulled down my shorts and sat on the bench, setting the towel beside me. I spread my legs and my cock stood straight up. Kiya looked at it, her mouth open, her eyes as large as dinner plates. I grabbed her, spun her around, kept her legs together, and sat her on my lap. She put her hands on my knees and forced her pussy against my cock. She was soaked, and she slid up and down on me, relishing my thickness.

"Do you think it will fit?" She whispered.

"I'll make it fit."

Her ass squished on my thighs with my cock poking out of her crack was a sight to behold. I pushed her up and angled my dick towards her entrance. She sat on me slowly; the tip disappeared inside her, and she yelped.

She sat, frozen in place, shocked I was finally inside her. I slowly applied pressure downwards, gripping her hips tight.

"Oh. My. Goooooooddd." She moaned from her soul. "It's stretching me, fuuuuuck."

Her lips enveloped me, and I saw her sink onto me and stop halfway. She was squeezing me tighter than a fist, almost making my dick go numb.

"My dildo wasn't big enough." She whimpered.

"It's okay." I leaned forward and kissed her back. I grabbed her hips and lifted her up, watching her lips grip my cock. I slowly set her back down, then moved her up and down on me in rhythm. Her cream began to lather me, and inch by inch, I was able to coax her to sit all the way down. She sat on my lap, my cock completely inside her.

"It- it's so big." She whispered. "I can't- It's- all inside- I can't- I stretched to fit all of it." She was vibrating, visibly on the verge of orgasm.

"Of course. I'm going to fuck you, but I'm going to be gentle." I whispered low. "I think you're going to need the towel, though."

She nodded, and I handed it to her. As she put it in her mouth, I grabbed her hips and lifted her up, only an inch, then pressed her back down. She moaned gutturally into the towel. Her pussy gripped, her body shaked, and her second orgasm of the night rolled through her.

I sat her down on me over and over, listening to her moans and watching her cream collect at the base of my shaft, where her pussy settled after every pump. She became louder, squeezed me tighter, and couldn't stop convulsing. She spit out the towel.

"I'm cumming Daddy oh fuuuuck." She whispered. "I love your dick. I love your dick so much."

Something inside my head snapped.

I grabbed her arms by the elbows and cinched them behind her back, and she cried out in pain. I stood up and held her bent over by her arms and slid my cock out of her, then slammed back inside. She screamed out and quivered. I started to fuck her with my entire length, punishing her with my cock.

"Oh- oh- fu- uk- I'm- cu- um- ing- ing- Da- aa- ddy- yy—" She cried. I lost count of how many times she came.

I watched my cock disappear inside of her over and over, then saw her cream collect rapidly over it.

"I'm leaking!" She shrieked, her voice an octave higher. "It's- it's- it's spilling on the flo- oor—"

Her cream had begun to flow freely, dripping on my shoes and the gym linoleum floor. I started increasing my pace, feeling my cum well inside me. I was animalistic, consumed by the need to consume her. She was the object of my carnal desire, and I was relentless in my quest to fuck her in half.

Her head fell down, her body limp, and I supported her entire weight, my fucking the only thing keeping her upright. She mumbled in a low voice, barely coherent.

What is she saying?

"Iloveyourdickiloveyourdickilove—"

"I'm going to cum. I can't stop." I growled, desperate for release. I fucked her harder and harder, forcing my weight into her ass, pounding her body outwards, then yanking her back onto me with every thrust.

"BREED ME, DADDY." She screamed at the top of her lungs with the last of her energy. "FUCK YOUR CUM INTO ME—"

I exploded inside of her, my cum penetrating the vacuum of her womb as her pussy spasmed, drawing my cum in further as I fucked it deeper.

"Oh fuck." She whimpered, barely conscious. I pumped myself into her slowly until I was content that my cum had filled her completely.

I released her arms one by one, and held her in an embrace as my dick became smaller. I pulled out of her and miraculously, she kept all of my cum inside her, squeezing her legs together.

Just then, we heard the gym door chime.

Chapter Five

The front door chime of the gym rang.

I was filled with adrenaline instantly. Before Kiya could react, I squatted down, grabbed her shorts, and yanked them back onto her. I snatched up the towel and quickly cleaned myself, my shoes, then mopped up her cum off the floor.

"I'll get out of the bathroom first," I whispered urgently. "I'm going to pretend I'm doing an exercise. You leave the bathroom a few minutes after me, get your stuff, then leave to your car. I'll follow you after a while."

She nodded, frightened. I moved towards the front of the locker room and peered out the exit. I couldn't see anyone, so I quietly left, then walked back to the bench I had been using. At the bench press area, I saw a young guy in sweats and a hoodie fighting late-night demons. It didn't look like he had seen me. I decided I might as well do a few shoulder burnout sets and picked up some lighter weights.

I watched as Kiya left the bathroom, and she looked completely normal. She picked up her stuff and went through the front door. I looked over and saw the young guy checking out her ass as she walked away and grinned to myself. After a few minutes, I decided I was done, grabbed my stuff, and walked out.

That could've been bad.

I met Kiya at our cars in the parking lot.

"You okay?" I asked.

She nodded. "That was hot. We almost... We almost—"

"I know," I said and grinned.

"I have to take a test tomorrow; I need to go home and study something so I don't bomb."

"Okay." I kissed her on the cheek, and she leaned in to hug me. "I'll see you at your game tomorrow. Good luck on your test."

"Thank you!" She said happily.

We got into our respective vehicles. I watched her leave safely, then headed back to my apartment. When I arrived, I made some food for myself, sat in bed, and wondered what Monday would bring.

In the morning, I stopped by to get the coffee order and was disappointed that Kiya wasn't there.

Right. She's taking a test.

When I got to work and walked into Amanda's office, she immediately interrogated me for details about my night with Kiya. I feigned reluctance, then spilled.

"Oh, wow." She said, impressed. "You are a naughty boy."

I grinned. "I won't be able to stay late today. Kiya has a basketball game."

"That's fine." She nodded. "We should get started, then."

The next few hours were somehow even worse than Friday's lessons, and my head was beginning to split open from information. A human mind is only supposed to comprehend so much at once, and mine was not doing so well.

"I feel so dumb," I said, stressed. "I understand why it's supposed to work; I just don't get how it does."

Amanda stood and put her hand on my shoulder. "It's fine, baby. I have to use the restroom. Just relax for a while, and we'll come back to it."

I nodded as she pushed through the entrance of her secret bathroom. Then, I heard a knock at the office door, and Gordon cracked it open.

"Hey, bud, got a sweet little lady here to see you." He chirped.

Kiya? Here?

I was unprepared for their meeting today, and Kiya's presence struck lightning through my body. I nodded at Gordon and walked to the door. Kiya thanked Gordon, then walked into the office. She was wearing leggings and a shirt that said 'BABYMETAL'.

"Hi, Mark." She said, strangely sweet. "I didn't get to see you this morning 'cause of my test, so I wanted to bring you one." She handed me a coffee and smiled.

I smiled back. "Hey. How was the test?"

She shrugged. "It was fine. Where's your boss?" She asked pointedly.

I knew she wouldn't let the car thing go.

"She, uh, went to the bathroom," I said.

"She?"

Oh boy.

I nodded. "Yeah."

Kiya breathed in, then acted unbothered. "Wow, this office is huge. There's a ton of cool shit in here, too."

She walked over to the desk, investigated the papers on top, and then walked back towards me. She opened her mouth to say something when she was interrupted.

"Hello. You must be Kiya." Amanda appeared in the doorway of the secret bathroom.

Amanda wore a provocative black blouse with deep cleavage showing and a short checkered wool skirt all morning. Her attire was part of the reason I couldn't focus. Kiya stared at her, mouth agape.

"You- I knew it!" She said loudly, nearly yelling. "The 'other woman' is your boss! You're fucking your—"

Amanda strode across the room in the blink of an eye and materialized in front of her.

"Yes." She uttered, her voice dripping with dominance as she cut off Kiya. "Let's keep that a secret between us, shall we?"

Amanda was only two inches taller than Kiya, yet she towered above the younger woman, who cowered before her, instinctively submitting.

"Yes," Kiya whispered, terrified. "I'm sorry—"

"Amanda." She stepped back and outstretched her hand. "It's so good to finally meet you."

Kiya was holding her breath but shook her hand. She looked at me quizzically. "Mark talks about me?"

"Oh yes. You're even prettier than he described."

Kiya blushed. "Thank you."

"I love your shirt." Amanda praised. "You have good taste in music, darling."

Kiya's trepidation and jealousy vanished, and she eagerly gushed about music with Amanda. After several minutes, she paused and checked her phone.

"Fuck, I'm gonna be late to work, I have to go. Bye, Miss Amanda." She said as she started walking towards the door.

"Drive safe, Kiya," Amanda said. She nodded at me towards Kiya.

I gave her a weak smile in apology, followed, and walked Kiya through the building and out to the parking lot, back to her car. After her encounter, she seemed to be struggling to form a sentence.

"Why- I mean- You—" She stuttered. We stopped at her car, and she took a breath. "That's like a whole ass wife in there. Why are you hanging out with... me?"

I shrugged. "She's the one who gave me the confidence to talk to you in the first place."

"Really?" She was shocked. "Does... Does she give you Mommy vibes too?"

I burst out laughing. "Mommy vibes is kind of an understatement."

She looked back at the office with a dreamy expression. Then she snapped back to reality, opened her car door, pulled out a ticket, and handed it to me.

"I got you a courtside seat!" She said happily.

"Awesome." I smiled. "Am I allowed to tell the other team that they're bad and they should feel bad?"

She giggled at my dumb joke. "No, be nice."

"Fine-uh." I acted annoyed and kissed her on the cheek. "See you then."

When I walked back into Amanda's office, she was staring off into space, sitting at her desk, and her eyes were red from crying. Panic shot through me.

"A- Amanda? What's wrong?" I asked, worried.

She didn't meet my eyes. She looked down at her desk and shuffled papers without purpose. "I can see... Kiya is very special. I'm sure she will make you happy. I know that I... I won't..."

She's leaving you. Because you're getting closer with Kiya.

"Wait—" I whispered, my voice caught in my constricted throat. I couldn't breathe. My knees weakened, and my heart collapsed.

"I won't... I won't get in your way, Sweetie." She said, her voice weak and defeated. She looked at me. Her mouth was smiling, but her eyes were empty and tortured. "You deserve to be happy with each other."

If she's done, you might as well wrap that fancy car of yours around a telephone pole and get it over with.

"Please don't leave me," I croaked, barely able to form words. Tears trickled down my face. "I don't want to be hollow again."

"What?" She whispered.

I fell to my knees. My body was drained, my soul snatched to the ether. When Amanda saw me fall, she leapt out of her chair, rushed around the desk, and dropped to her knees before me. She cupped my face in her hands.

"Baby, you should be with someone your own age." She reasoned. "You shouldn't be trapped with me."

I shook my head. " I don't need Kiya like I need you." I whimpered. "I'm supposed to be yours. I'm meant to be yours."

She pressed her forehead to mine. "What about Kiya? You like her, don't you?"

"Of course but..." I took a breath and said what was true. "I don't love her like I love you."

AMANDA'S MARK 69

"What did you say?" Her voice was tender and afraid.

I raised my head and peered into her eyes.

"I love you, Amanda. I love you, Mommy." My voice cracked, and I cleared my throat. "I don't have to see Kiya anymore. I don't need anyone else. I'll do anything. Don't make me go. Please—"

Amanda pulled me into a kiss. Our souls intertwined, and I tasted my fate on her tongue.

"I love you too, Mark." She whispered after we took a breath. "I won't let you go. You belong to me."

I began shifting on the floor uncomfortably, my cock was fully erect, spurred on by our intimacy. Amanda noticed, then reached into my lap and touched me.

"I might have to keep Kiya around, if only to keep this thing from wearing me through." She giggled.

I looked at her quizzically.

"How about I take all of us to dinner tonight, after her basketball game. I think we can come to an understanding." She said warmly.

"Okay," I whispered. "I love you." The taste of those words on my lips was intoxicating.

"I love you too, sweet boy."

The rest of the day passed quickly, and Amanda had me leave work early so I could pick up flowers to give to Kiya after her game.

After picking out a beautiful bouquet, I drove to the stadium, parked, and sat courtside to watch the game. Kiya and her teammates played ferociously. She made sure I watched when she scored points, and the teammates I had met the day earlier also kept a close eye on me.

She must've told them about our 'gym session'.

It was a close and competitive game, but Kiya's team squeezed out a narrow victory. After the final buzzer, I stood up and cheered her. She was ecstatic, ran to me, and nearly jumped into my arms.

"We did it! I can't believe we did it." She said, breathless. "We always lose to them."

Shayna, Lin, and Mindy walked over to where we were standing. Shayna gave me a seductive smile.

"You must be our good luck charm." She drawled.

"Congratulations, ladies." I smiled. I reached under my seat, picked up the flowers I was hiding, and handed them to Kiya. "You deserve the win."

Kiya took them, beaming, and smelled their fresh scent. Shayna looked at me knowingly.

"Have fu-unnn." She sang as she and the other girls walked away.

Kiya was jumping up and down, happy with her victory flowers. I grabbed her hand.

"Amanda wants to take us to dinner to celebrate your game," I said tentatively.

"Oh, okay!" She said. She seemed very pleased with that idea. "Where are we going?"

"It's some fancy place I haven't heard of; I'm not rich enough to know about it."

"Swanky." She said, swaying her hips. "Can you give me a ride home so I can shower and get ready?"

"Absolutely," I said, smiling.

On the way to her place, we discussed how the game went. I had never been into basketball, so I wasn't very familiar with the rules. She ran me through how everything worked. I didn't understand much, but thankfully, we arrived at her apartment before I got too confused. She unlocked the door and brought me inside, and I saw she was an excellent interior decorator. The place was modest but very artsy and cute. She had several houseplants that livened up the living room. She pointed to the green cloth couch set up in front of the TV.

"You can chill on the couch; I'll try to be quick!" She chimed as she ran to her bedroom. I heard the shower turn on.

I found the TV remote, plopped down on the couch, turned on the TV, and looked up a YouTube video essay I'd meant to watch. I liked watching video essays about games or shows I didn't have the time to play or watch. About twenty minutes in, I heard the shower turn off.

That was quick.

Kiya's faint footsteps padded the floor, and suddenly, she was standing between me and the TV. Her hair was wet, and her lithe body was wrapped in a white plush towel. It barely covered her breasts, and it stopped at the top of her thighs. I could almost see everything. My pants immediately got tight.

She waited until I finished gazing at her and met my eyes. She dropped the towel and stepped towards the couch. She stood in front of me, leaned over, and kissed me while she unbuckled my pants. She rushed, pulled my pants around my knees, then dropped her legs on either side of me and straddled my lap. She resumed kissing me as she slid her pussy against my cock.

"Please, Daddy. Fuck me before we go. I need your dick." She whimpered.

Without waiting for an answer, she reached her hand down and positioned me at her entrance. She sat down hard, taking me halfway.

"Oh fuck." She moaned, and she wrapped her arms around my head and pressed my face into her small breasts.

I wasn't in any position to say no. I slid my hands around her hips and grabbed her tight ass, lifted her up, then gently brought her back down onto me. She gyrated her hips, easing me deep inside her. After a few moments, her pussy accepted all of me, and she sat firmly on my cock.

"It feels so good inside me." She moaned into my ear.

"You couldn't help yourself, could you?" I whispered back. "You're such a little slut."

She whimpered, and I felt her cream seep onto me as her walls relaxed around my dick. I kissed her deeply and raised her gently up and down myself. She was a human fuckdoll, and I fucked her body onto me slowly. I enjoyed the sensation, the conversation between our bodies. I made her cum twice, sweet little orgasms as she trembled and whimpered into me. I could stay suspended inside of her forever.

"Are you gonna cum?" She asked, after she recovered from her third orgasm.

I shook my head. My cock didn't want to cum. It wanted to slowly salivate precum inside her, while her tight pussy massaged cream into my skin.

"Daddy." She whined. "I'm gonna make us late to dinner. Punish me. Punish me with your dick and breed me."

Fuck her senseless.

Her coaxing worked. "Wrap your arms around my neck, or you're going to fall," I growled.

She did as I told her, then I slid one arm under her leg, pushed my other arm against the couch, and stood up. My pants fell to my ankles, and I deftly kicked them off my feet. I steadied my other arm under her leg and supported her whole weight, her legs folded over my elbows. I grabbed her ass tight with both hands, lifted her almost all the way off me, then slammed her down the entire length of my cock. Her body impacted me with a wet slap, and she screamed into my ear. I spoke firmly back.

"You." Slap.

"Are." Slap.

"Such." Slap.

"A." Slap.

"Fucking." Slap.

"Whore." Slap.

Her body couldn't process the intensity, so it compensated by sending her into a continuous orgasm. She came nonstop, moaning loudly, for several minutes as I stood with her perched in my arms, pounding her with murderous intent. Her cream was spattered on my stomach and coated the floor, and her screams echoed in the apartment. I was beginning to get close to cumming when I noticed her screams turning into sobs. Her pussy was less wet, and my dick no longer effortlessly penetrated her, it was met with friction. She was drying up and crying in pain. I had given her too much.

I slowed and stopped, her head fell against my shoulder, and tears streamed down my chest.

"Shhh. I'm sorry, baby, I'm sorry." I whispered. I eased her off of me, turned, and set her down on the couch. When I let go, I saw something amazing.

I held her as she lay naked on the couch. She was still crying, and her body twitched, spasmed uncontrollably every couple seconds.

"Are you still cumming?" I asked, incredulous.

She nodded. Her sobs lessened, and soon she was able to speak.

"That was so good." She whimpered.

"I'm so sorry. I felt you getting dry..." I said.

"No, it was so hot." She interrupted. "My pussy just hurts so much, I'm still sore from yesterday."

I nodded.

We did go from 0 to 100 pretty quickly.

She took a deep, rasping breath. "I'm okay. I promise. That was so fucking good. That was... mind-shattering." She reassured me. "You didn't cum though." She pouted.

I shook my head. "That's fine. If I had kept going, I would've torn you. It's okay, really."

She still looked disappointed, but she quickly collected herself. "Okay. For real, I need to get ready. I'm gonna pass out if I don't eat something."

I nodded in agreement, and she stood and then went to the bedroom. I collected my pants, put them back on, then fixed myself in the mirror. I was still wearing my work suit, but I couldn't return to my apartment and change, or we would be late. After ten minutes, Kiya came back from her bedroom. She looked fantastic. She wore tight black jeans, a fancy yellow top that complimented her skin, simple makeup, and natural poofy hair. She looked like the sun, and I was blinded.

"This is all I could do 'cause we're gonna be late." She snapped as she hurriedly put on earrings.

"You look exquisite, babe," I said.

She gave me a warm smile, and then we rushed to the car. Thankfully, the drive to the restaurant was short, but parking was a nightmare. We drove around three square blocks, hunting for a spot, until I realized something.

"Wait a second," I muttered.

"What?" Kiya asked.

"I'm gonna try something," I said.

I drove back to the restaurant and parked in front of it. A valet had decided my sleek black sports car was worthy and came out to receive my keys. I handed them to him, got out, opened Kiya's door, and escorted her inside, grinning.

The restaurant was speakeasy-themed and very classy. There were cloths on the tables, paintings on the walls, and upper-class attire all around. I was overwhelmed, but feeling Kiya cling to me, overwhelmed as well, gave me courage, and we charged forward.

An attendant stood at a podium near the front door. "Mr. Sampson?"

"Y- yes." I replied, taken aback.

"Right this way, please." The attendant led us to a table where Amanda was waiting. She still had her work clothes on as I did, but she was as radiant as ever. I pulled a chair out for Kiya, let her sit, and then sat down myself.

"Such wonderful manners." Amanda purred.

"Isn't that what all guys do?" I quipped.

"No. Not all men do what you do, darling." Amanda said as Kiya shook her head.

"Oh," I said, smiling as I looked down.

AMANDA'S MARK

We looked over our menus and ordered our drinks.

"You look stunning, sweetie. How was the game?" Amanda asked.

"Thank you." Kiya beamed. "I don't know how we won, but we pulled it off. My teammates say it's because we were motivated by Mark." She giggled. "We've never been able to beat that team until today."

"You all wanted to impress him," Amanda said, smiling.

"It worked." I shrugged. "They were badass."

Kiya blushed.

After our drinks had been delivered, the waiter took our order. I wanted to leave Kiya and Amanda alone, so I excused myself to use the bathroom. I wondered what Amanda would say, and I had no idea if Kiya would be on board with whatever she was planning. After I used the bathroom, I walked back toward the table. I saw the two ladies engaged in what appeared to be a thrilling conversation, so I decided not to interrupt them.

I found a dartboard on the wall and gave it a shot. After three rounds, I concluded that I wasn't very good at darts. I was beginning to get frustrated when a large Black butch woman in a full suit with cropped hair struck up conversation with me.

"How's it going?" She nodded over to my table. "Took your girl out to meet your mom?"

"Something like that." I laughed. "My, um, girlfriend, I guess, is meeting my... Uh, other... Girlfriend."

"Damn dude." She laughed. "You must slang dick harder than me."

"With your build?" I replied and shook my head. "Ain't no way."

She chuckled and extended her hand. "I'm Pat. P for short."

I smiled, and we exchanged a firm handshake. "Hey P, I'm Mark."

"So you have a thruple thing going on?"

I shook my head. "I have no idea, honestly. I'm just having an amazing time, and I..." I sighed. "I don't wanna fuck anything up."

She nodded. "That's honest, at least. Most guys would be bragging. Hell, I'd be bragging. They're fine as fuck."

I laughed. "I don't have anything to brag about; I didn't do anything. I don't even know how I got here."

She thought for a second. "You probably got here because you treat those girls how they should be treated."

"Huh," I said. "Maybe my purpose in life is just to please women." I threw another dart, and it expertly missed the board and lodged into the wall.

Pat laughed. "Hell, I'm the same way, brother." She clapped me on the shoulder. "No shit." She said suddenly, amazed.

I saw she was looking back at my table. I looked over and saw that Amanda had pulled Kiya in. They were passionately kissing, and Kiya melted into Amanda's embrace.

"Whoa." I went to the wall, pulled the dart out, and set the darts back into the board. "It was nice to meet you, Pat."

She gave me a big grin as I walked away. "Nice to meet you too, Mark."

When I got back to the table, Amanda looked hungry for something other than food, and Kiya was flushed. "Hey. Did I miss anything?"

Amanda gave me a devious look. "I think we figured things out."

"Oh." I smiled and looked at Kiya. She smiled at me sheepishly, blushing.

I sat back down just in time for the food to be delivered. The food was delicious, but I had difficulty focusing on eating after a few minutes. Both Amanda and Kiya took advantage of the tablecloth, slipped their feet out of their shoes, and played footsie in my lap. They giggled and laughed like it was an inside joke, and I smiled and tried to keep eating. I was thankful they didn't have the dexterity to release my dick from my pants, and I was hard as a rock trying to keep my composure.

AMANDA'S MARK

After our plates were clean, Amanda spoke up. "Let's go to my house and have some more drinks. We could play a game or two." She said.

"Oh? What kind of game, Miss Amanda?" Kiya said, a little too innocently.

"I was thinking blackjack." She replied, a grin on her face.

There's another game I'm terrible at.

Amanda paid the bill and we left together. The valet brought her Cadillac first, then my Corvette. She took the highway route, and I followed.

She wants to race.

"Hold on," I said.

"What?" Kiya asked, nervous.

Amanda lined up next to me, and we hovered at 80mph. We waited until the road beyond us was clear, and she honked three times. I slammed on the gas, and Kiya and I were both thrown back into the seat.

"Oh my goooddd!" Kiya yelled as we accelerated quickly.

Amanda's supercharged SUV kept up with me until I reached 100mph, and then I blew her out of the water. I was several car lengths ahead when I reached 130mph, and then I let off the gas, having won. Amanda pulled in behind me, and we cruised together to her house.

"Holy shit. I didn't know this thing could do that." Kiya was breathless.

I grinned. "Were you scared or horny?"

She rubbed her thighs together. "Both."

Our race cut serious time off our commute, and soon we pulled into Amanda's driveway. We met her at the door; she unlocked it and led us in. We gathered around her minibar as she made us drinks, and then she set us up at a square table in the dining area. She brought out a silver case containing a few card decks and a poker chip set.

"What are we playing for?" I asked, playing with my chips as Amanda dealt our first hand.

Amanda and Kiya grinned, looking at each other and then at me. "Clothes!" they said in unison.

"I am so bad at this game," I said, defeated.

I had lost every single hand since we started playing and was now sitting at the table stark naked. Kiya and Amanda were looking at each other and me and giggling. They both remained fully clothed.

"So, now what? I lost this hand, but I don't have any clothes left to take off." I said, slightly annoyed.

Amanda stood up from the table. "Oh, sweetie, we'll just add clothes then."

Add clothes?

She sauntered behind me, then I felt fabric over my forehead, and darkness fell on my eyes. She had blindfolded me. She took my hand and helped me out of the chair.

"Come." She ordered. I followed.

She led me to what I assumed was the bedroom. I heard giggling and clothes being tossed on the floor. I heard a drawer open and close and the bed squeak. After a few moments, Kiya began moaning softly. Then, I felt Amanda's ass press against me. I reached down and felt her cheeks, then slid my hand down her slit and pushed a finger inside her. She was already soaking wet, and I heard her muffled moan.

"Good boy." She said, her voice faint. "But Mommy doesn't want your finger, she wants your cock."

I was more than happy to oblige. I removed my finger, lathered my cock with her pussy juice, then rubbed it up and down her slit. I found her entrance easily, then slid myself all the way inside her slowly. She moaned as my cock filled her up, and I heard Kiya whimper and gasp.

As far as I could tell, I was standing on the edge of the bed, fucking Amanda doggystyle, while she ate Kiya's pussy. I was frustrated that I couldn't see the two of them, but I was still more than happy to fuck my Mommy's pussy while she tongued my girlfriend.

I heard Kiya squeal in orgasm, and then Amanda came up for air. "Deep and steady, darling. I'm preparing this little girl for your perfect cock."

Isn't she still sore?

My dick surged and twitched, spilling a squirt of precum inside her. "Yes, Mommy," I grunted and groaned as I fucked her slow and deep, her pussy sent shivers down my spine and I wondered how long I would last.

I heard Kiya reach another shuddering orgasm and scream. "Oh FUCK- ungh- Fuck it's- it's so big." She whimpered.

"Yes baby, but get used to it because your Daddy is bigger." Amanda cooed.

"Oh fuck." Kiya whined in fear.

"Holy fuck I'm- I'm so close." Hearing them talk and Amanda's wet walls were sending me over the edge.

"No," Amanda stated. She moved off of me suddenly, then turned around and grabbed my dick hard at the base, sealing my orgasm inside me.

I stood, panting, her hand squeezed so hard it hurt. "Fuck." I whispered. "I'm sorry, Mommy, you just feel so good."

"It's okay, baby boy." She purred and slowly released her hand. I pushed, the pressure inside was easing and I spurted a single rope of cum. She placed her tongue under my tip and caught everything in her mouth.

"Oh, god." I whimpered. "It's still- I still need to—" I stammered.

"Shhh." She whispered. I felt her get up and off the bed.

She moved around behind me, and her hands untied the blindfold. When I opened my eyes, I saw Kiya laid on her back on the bed, an angled pillow beneath her hips lifting her ass, and a large buttplug fitted inside her.

I couldn't speak; I just stared with my mouth open.

"This little girl wants you to breed her, but her pussy was murdered by your fat cock." Amanda whispered into my ear, pouting. "It needs a rest. So you're going to impregnate her ass instead."

"But- I can't—" I said.

"Get her pregnant by fucking her ass?" She interrupted. "You should still try." She giggled.

Her voice made my cock twitch, and I hurriedly climbed onto the bed in front of Kiya. She had her legs pulled back, almost behind her head, and she stared at the ceiling. I grabbed the base of the plug and gently began pulling it out.

"Oh fuck." She cried.

I slowly worked it out of her until it suddenly popped and came free. She grunted with relief. Her ass was slightly gaping open from the size of the plug.

Just the right size for my tongue.

Without hesitation I plunged my tongue inside her ass, pushing deeper and deeper, face fucking her hole.

"FUCK DADDY." She screamed. My nose embedded itself into her pussy and cream collected on my face. "Oh my god, your tongue- I'm gonna- cuuuuummmm." She let out a deep sigh as her orgasm rushed through her.

I pulled my tongue out and my face away and saw Amanda was kneeling beside us, holding a squirt bottle of lube. She pumped twice into Kiya's gaping hole, which had been stretched slightly bigger by my tongue. Then she squirted some on my cock, and started stroking me up and down.

"Give her what she deserves, baby." She whispered.

She lined up my cock with Kiya's asshole and rested the tip inside. I leaned forward, and the head of my dick disappeared past her anal ring. Kiya gasped with a huge breath.

Her ass was ten times tighter than her pussy, which had nearly cut the circulation off my dick when I first fucked her. I eased in slightly, and she winced. I pulled it slightly out, and back and forth massaged her ring with the head of my dick, willing her to relax. Amanda began playing with her clit, rubbing it in fast circles. Soon, Kiya began moaning deeply.

"Oh, Daddy." She groaned. "Daddy, I want all of it."

"Push. Push Daddy's cock out of you." Amanda ordered.

Kiya gave her a quizzical look but began pushing. Her pussy leaked cream down to my dick, and suddenly her ass accepted half my cock. Kiya screamed in pleasure.

"FUCK OH FUCK—"

I fell forward, surprised, and shot my hand out to support myself. It wrapped around her throat and silenced her mid-scream. I looked down at her face. Her makeup was ruined; tears had destroyed it. Her hair was messy, and her eyes looked at me in fear.

"You look so pretty with my cock in your ass." I cooed to her. "You're such a perfect little whore."

Her eyes rolled into the back of her head, and a moan from the depths of her lungs escaped her mouth.

"Oh," Amanda said, surprised. Her hand was still between us, her fingers inside Kiya's pussy, and her thumb massaging her clit. "Oh my god, baby girl, you're squirting! You're squirting from Daddy fucking your ass!" She said, excited.

I felt her fluid trickle down to my cock, and I released her throat. I leaned back, grabbed her thighs from the front, and fucked her asshole against my cock. I slid her halfway down my length before pushing her forward and back again. Her small, steady river of squirt was lubricating my dick as it penetrated her.

"I'm fucking your squirt and cream back inside you," I growled. "I'm fucking your cum into your ass you filthy fucking slut."

Kiya was now catatonic; her head lolled backwards, her mouth gaped, her moans uncontrollable. She twitched and spasmed, remaining in a perpetual orgasm. Suddenly, I heard snoring, and the resistance her ass was giving my cock ceased. I slid all the way inside her, filling her anal passage completely.

You fucked her to sleep.

I was so close. I slowly fucked my entire length inside her asshole, penetrating to the absolute depth and sitting inside her, pulsing back and forth.

"I'm so fucking close. It's leaking out of me. Oh my fucking god she's so tight. Mommy her ass is so fucking tight on my dick." I moaned.

Amanda retrieved her hand from Kiya's pussy, and slapped her face. Kiya jolted awake into orgasm, her cheek wet with squirt, and she wailed.

"Do you want it, baby?" Amanda asked her sweetly.

"Please—" She cried. "PLEASE DADDY cum in my ass pleaaaaseee."

I pulled her thighs against me as hard as I could, and fell over the edge, flooding her ass with cum. She clenched my cock and shuddered, whimpering.

"C- c- cum- mmm- mmminngg—"

She instantly began snoring again. I pumped her asshole ten more times, forcing and plunging my cum inside her. After my orgasm passed, I gently pulled my shrinking cock away. It slid out quickly, and I saw her ass gaping, seeping my semen onto the pillow.

I sat back on my legs, exhausted. "What do we—?" I asked, gesturing to Kiya.

Amanda jumped out of bed, ran to the bathroom, and returned with two small towels. She placed the towel between Kiya's legs, covering her pussy and ass. Then, she pulled her legs together, keeping the towel in place.

"Help me." She gestured to Kiya, now in the fetal position, fast asleep.

I picked Kiya up off the bed, cradling her in my arms. Amanda used the other towel to wipe off the pillow and the bed underneath. It was still soaked, but she got the majority of it. Then, she pulled back the covers and nodded to the center of the bed.

"But, shouldn't we—" I asked.

Amanda interrupted. "No. She wants to wake up dirty, sore, and used." She said matter-of-factly.

I nodded. I put Kiya on the bed, her head resting on a pillow, and brought the sheets up to her chin. Amanda bent over and kissed her tenderly on the cheek.

"Good girl."

Amanda and I walked to the bathroom, where she turned on the shower and pulled me in for a kiss.

"That was hot. You are such a fucking stud." She said in disbelief.

"So, is this the arrangement you two agreed with?" I asked as I fidgeted with my dick, swelling back up.

She looked down at my dick, beginning to grow large again. "Yes... You belong to me, and she belongs to you. Pretty simple, actually."

She put her hand on her hip and looked at me like I was crazy. "Are you really trying to go again?"

I shrugged. "I don't know if I can cum again, but I can definitely fuck after a few minutes."

She pointed. "Get in the shower."

She methodically cleaned me, giving special consideration to my aching dick. Even though she was very gentle, soon I was rock hard again. It hurt. My cock was in pain after fucking Kiya's virgin ass, but I couldn't be bothered. Amanda finished rinsing me off, then embraced me, her wet soaking body pressing against mine.

"You ready, cowboy?" She purred.

"Are you? You're riding, Mommy." I replied.

I reached under her legs, caught her knees with my elbows, and picked her up. She was a little heavier than Kiya, so I pushed her against the shower wall and held her there. She kissed me deeply as I reached down and guided my cock into her. I eased her down onto me, fully, completely, totally, absolutely.

We stood there making love in the shower for ages. We barely moved, I bobbed her up and down lightly, she squeezed my cock, I twitched and pulsed it back. We were eternally each other's. She came countless times, all of them gentle and delicate. Every time she whispered into my ear, inspired by the orgasms permeating her.

"I'm cumming on your perfect cock."

"I love you. You're mine."

"You're God's favorite. You're my favorite."

"Mommy needs your dick. Mommy needs you."

"You're such a good boy."

"I- I- Oh my god, I love you, Mark."

Her last orgasm was heavy and deep; it penetrated her soul as I penetrated her. Making her cum, the gentle friction on my aching cock, and her tender words were pushing me over the edge. I felt it boil inside of me, craving release into my lover.

"I- I- You- Your pussy feels like the walls of heaven." I stuttered, whispering. "I'm so close Mommy. You're gonna make me cum again."

"Put me down, Sweetie." She said, having recovered.

I lifted her up, and set her feet back down on the tiled floor. She reached for the bottle of conditioner, then slid down and squatted on the floor. She poured conditioner onto her hand and lathered it around her breasts, then onto my cock. I was so sensitive that the feeling nearly caused me to collapse. She smiled and giggled. I threw my hands up against the wall to support myself.

She placed my dick gingerly between her breasts, then cupped her hands over her nipples and squeezed. Her full breasts against her palms caused magnificent ripples in the flesh, and I gazed in amazement. Her endowments slipped and slid around my cock, making me squirm and seize. She jiggled them up and down, then alternated, playing with them and me.

I dropped my head against the wall and stared down at her. "Oh my fucking god." I whimpered.

"Cum! Cum! Cum for me!!" She said eagerly. "Cum for Mommy!!"

She looked down at her chest and opened her mouth right as I erupted. She continued to manipulate her breasts, milking my cock as my cum jetted into her mouth. She caught three spurts and swallowed, the rest showering down into her cleavage.

"Good boy!" She said happily. "Mommy loves making you cum."

I nearly fell against the wall; I was so spent. I leaned back against the wall, then helped Amanda up. She quickly washed and rinsed her chest. We shared one more loving kiss, and then we got out and dried off.

We crawled into bed, and Kiya was sound asleep between us. I fell into slumber, peaceful, content, and loved.

Chapter Six

"Fuck! Oh fuck!"

Kiya.

My eyes snapped open when I heard her screaming. I sat up, half asleep, and panicked.

"What- what's wrong—"

"Oh my goooooddd." Kiya cried. The sheets over her were moving; she was propped up against the headboard and moaning towards the ceiling.

She was intently, furiously masturbating. Amanda jolted awake, sat up, noticed Kiya, and smiled.

"You passed out and Daddy filled your ass with cum." She purred sleepily. "Do you feel it? Do you feel his cum in your ass?"

"I feel it." Kiya whimpered. "Daddy, I love your cuuu- uuu- uuummm." Her orgasm ran through her in waves, and she sank back into the bed, content.

"Oh, wow," I whispered. "Did you like waking up sore, used, and filled?"

She leaned her head towards me, pursed her lips, and nodded affectionately. "Good girl," I said, then leaned over and kissed her tenderly.

I slid my hand under the covers, palmed her small breasts, and tweaked her pierced nipples. She moaned into my mouth, and then I pushed my hand down, caressing her stomach before landing in her lap. I spread her pussy lips gently and my finger found her clit, and I rubbed circles into it, using her fresh cum as lubricant. She clung to my arm, squeezing me into her, and clamped her muscular thighs around my hand. She started whimpering into my kiss faster and faster, and just before she climaxed, I broke the kiss.

"Be a good girl and cum for me again," I murmured.

Her thighs crushed my hand in a vice-like grip, and she spasmed, bucking back and forth in the bed as she came. She kept her lips shut and peered up at me with doe eyes.

"Mmm- mmm- mmuhh- ohhhhhhh." She finally gasped.

Her thighs released my hands. "Thank you, Daddy." She muttered, her energy settling back down to normal. "I have to go to school, ugh!" She whined, pouting. "Thank you, Miss Amanda. I have to go home and clean up."

"Of course, Darling." Amanda cooed. She was lying on her side, her thighs rubbed together lazily.

She enjoyed the show.

Kiya pushed up the covers and clambered out of bed, then searched the floor for items of her clothing. She quickly put them back on, then tied her shoes barefoot, opting not to put dirty socks back on.

"I'll see you later!! That was—" She paused, looking up and remembering. "Nope. Can't. I need to go!" She rushed out of the bedroom and closed the door.

Amanda looked ready to devour me. "Breakfast?" She asked innocently.

I nodded eagerly. She threw back the covers, spun around on all fours, then slammed her pussy into my face. I hungrily ate her, lapping her wetness. She grabbed my cock and swallowed it whole as I found her clit. I grunted loudly into her pussy, my tip deep in her throat. She was aggressive, violently bobbing up and down my dick, and saliva streamed down my balls. I sucked her clit with the same fervor, flicking it rapidly with my tongue. Her pussy juice flowed readily down my chin, her thighs squeezed my head, and she grinded her pussy into my face. I felt our mutual orgasm building when suddenly, the bedroom door opened again.

"Hey," Kiya said, breathless from the view and embarrassed by her interruption. "Uh. Wow. Miss Amanda, you're so sexy, oh my god."

Amanda lifted her mouth from me. "Thank you, Sweetie."

"Um," Kiya said. "I- well- Mark gave me a ride..."

Amanda swung her leg over my head and lifted herself off. "Oh shit," I said, coming up for air. "You're right. Let me get ready."

I kissed Amanda deeply, hopped out of bed, and ran to the living room to fetch my clothes. I hurriedly put on my pants and button-down shirt from yesterday and threw on my shoes and belt, looking semi-presentable. Amanda came out of the bedroom in a black robe, fetched her keys, and went outside with us.

"Bye, you two." She said, kissing both of us on the cheek. "See you at work in a bit, baby." I nodded as she entered her SUV to move it into the street.

She pulled out as I opened the passenger door of the Vette for Kiya. She clambered in and smiled as I closed the door.

How did you get so lucky to be here?

I got in, pulled out, and drove to Kiya's apartment.

We were cruising down a side street when the car's display screen lit up with a phone number, and the default ringtone started playing.

'ALEXIS CALLING'

"Hah! No." I hung up immediately.

"Who is— Oh," Kiya said. She looked at me, clearly annoyed. "Why is she calling you?"

I shrugged. "Dunno. I thought she had a boyfriend now."

'ALEXIS CALLING'

The phone was ringing again. I stared at it for several seconds.

Why the fuck is my ex calling me?

I looked at Kiya. She shrugged. "Now I'm curious." She said.

I let it ring for a few more seconds, sighed, and hit the answer button. "Hey," I said, deadpan.

"H— — Mar— Sorr—" She voice was breaking up.

I couldn't hear what she was saying. She was outside; it was windy, and I thought I heard cars rushing past.

"Hey, I can't hear you at all."

I heard some muffling, and then her voice became clearer. She had cupped her hand to the bottom of the phone.

"Hey. Mark. Sorry, I— Can you— I need help. Please." She sounded frustrated.

"What's going on?" I replied.

"My tire went flat on the freeway, and my dad is out of town, my fucking boyfriend doesn't know how to change a fucking tire, I'm late to work, I know this is weird but I really need your help please." She rambled on. She was desperate, nearly on the verge of tears. I'd never heard her sound like this before.

Might as well. It's not that big of a deal.

I looked over to Kiya, who was listening to everything. She shrugged.

"Yeah, uh, I guess. Sure. Does your car have a spare and a jack kit? Mine doesn't; it just has a plug-in air compressor and sealant." I said.

"Yeah it does, I just don't know how to do any of this shit." She replied.

"Alright. I have to drop my girlfriend off at her place, then I'll stop by the store real quick and head to you. Send me your location pin. It'll probably be about twenty minutes until I get there."

She was quiet when I mentioned my girlfriend. After a few moments, she spoke softly: "Okay. Thank you, Mark."

"No problem." I hung up.

I looked over to Kiya, who was smiling broadly.

"Girlfriend??" She giggled.

I laughed. "Yes."

She smiled, and then her face got serious. "Listen. Be careful with her."

"What do you mean?"

"She's going to try to manipulate you. She's gonna see your fancy car and clothes and try to pounce. If you give her a chance, she'll take it. And more." She said knowingly.

I nodded.

I called Amanda and told her I would be late to work and why. She seemed very amused with the situation.

After I dropped Kiya off, I headed to an auto parts store between my and Alexis's locations. There, I bought a tire plug kit and a spray bottle. Thankfully, the employee let me fill the bottle with soapy water. Quickly, I headed toward where she was; I didn't want to make her wait too long.

She was sitting in a beige sedan on the side of the highway. I pulled in behind her and parked, then set my hazard lights. I waited until the lane was clear, then carefully exited the car. When Alexis saw me, she looked stunned, then slowly got out.

"Mark?" She asked, and looked me up and down.

Alexis was my height, very thin, and had dirty blonde hair. She was quite beautiful, but my time with her made me see an uglier side. When she got the flat, she was wearing scrubs and on her way to the hospital.

"Hey." I gave her a curt wave as I walked towards the car.

"You- you look completely different." She stuttered. "You used to be like... Skin and bones. Now you're..."

Her voice trailed off as she watched me roll up my sleeves and intently stare at my muscled forearms, her mouth slightly open, oblivious.

"Beefy?" I finished for her. "The breakup was great motivation. Also, I actually started eating. Instead of, y'know... Not."

This is awkward.

She looked down. "Which tire is it?" I asked.

"The right back one." She pointed.

"Can you get your jack kit out? I gotta grab the soap water."

She nodded and opened her trunk. She deliberately bent over with her legs straight, showing her ass. It was small but tight and perky. She wiggled it back and forth as she got out the jack kit.

Of course.

I turned to the other side of my car and grabbed the soapy water bottle and the plug kit. I set them down next to the tire and looked at it. It was completely deflated, and the rim was pressed against the pavement. She finally fished the jack kit out of the trunk and handed it to me. I squatted down next to the car and felt for the pinch point in front of the tire. When I found it, I slid the jack under and began jacking the car up.

"So who's this new girlfriend?" She asked without hesitation.

I sighed and continued rotating the jack mechanism. "Kiya—"

"Kiya Morris!?" She asked in disbelief.

I nodded.

"You're seriously giving that ratchet little girl rides in this—"

Ice ran through my veins. "Watch your fucking mouth," I spoke low, but with diction and power.

Alexis had heard me over the sound of traffic and froze. I'd never spoken to her that way in all our years together.

I paused, looked up at her, and gestured to the work I was doing. "Choose your next words carefully," I said simply.

She blinked and swallowed. She decided not to say anything, which I was fine with. I went back to my work. After the tire was acceptably off the ground, I sprayed it and spun it around, checking for the leak. After a minute, I found a shiny dot surrounded by foaming water.

I pointed at it and showed her. "There. It's just a nail. I can plug it here, air up the tire, and you'll be fine. Or I can put the spare on, and you can take it to a shop."

She hugged herself nervously. "I'm scared of driving on the highway on a donut."

I nodded. "Same here."

I needed to remove the tire since the nail was toward the far edge. Thankfully, the nuts came loose fairly easily and weren't wrenched down. After removing the wheel, I dug the nail out of the tire with one of the tools included in the kit. I cleaned the hole and forced the plug inside. I returned to my car, retrieved the air compressor, and filled the tire. Once it reached the standard psi, I sprayed the soap water back on it and found no more leaks. I put the wheel back on and hand-tightened the lugs. I released the jack slowly, and once the car set back down on the road, I used the wrench to torque down the nuts tighter by stepping on it. I caught Alexis staring at my ass.

Can't blame her; it does look good in slacks.

I stood up and turned around, and Alexis pressed herself against me and her car. She stared at me with demanding eyes.

"Let me take you out for a drink. As a thank you." Her voice was sweet, but I wasn't falling for it. Not anymore.

I shook my head no. "We're both seeing other people."

She leaned back with a pitched laugh. "So? They don't have to know."

I stared at her.

I remembered how I used to be head-over-heels for her, and she barely gave me the time of day. I doted on her and gave her as much of my sixteen-year-old self as possible. Nothing was ever enough to earn her attention. I was desperate for love, and she took advantage of me by dropping scraps of affection that I devoured like a starving dog.

A year later, when she took my virginity, she acted as though she had provided a divine service, as though surely no one else would be willing to stoop so low for me.

I remembered her wrath. I always had to remain available for her, but she didn't do the same for me. The few times I dared to ignore her back, the consequence was her sharp, spiteful tongue that sliced through my soul. I was worthless to her. Less than nothing. Yet she was everything to me, and I clung to her like a barnacle on a vessel.

At eighteen, I mustered my courage after graduation and told her I'd had enough. I wouldn't remain on her leash while she traipsed through college. She laughed in my face. I had done her a favor.

"You're pathetic." She spat at me. "You're a burger-flipping loser, and that's all you'll ever be. You couldn't even get into the free college!"

She knew. She knew I couldn't go to college and that I had to work full time to escape my home life, but she used that knowledge against me.

She walked away, her face consumed with pity and disgust.

If she hated you so much, why didn't she let you go until the end?

I stared at her.

"I just..." She leaned closer; her fingers trailed up my chest. "I wanted to thank you for helping me. I knew you'd come running again if I ever needed you to." Her lips played with a twisted smile.

This. Fucking. Bitch. Pop the spare and the other tire and leave her here. She REALLY fucking thinks SHE CAN JUST-

Hold on. What did Kiya say? She would jump at any chance?

I formulated a plan to bring her ego down a notch. If the world wasn't going to give her comeuppance, I might as well collect on what was due.

"I mean... How do you want to thank me?" I asked, feigning sheepishness.

"How do you think?" She stated, and she slipped her hand down to my crotch. My cock rose to her touch.

I oozed a smile, unable to contain my joy of what I had in mind for her. She smiled back, yet in her eyes I spied suspicion. She wasn't a fool, and I had folded too easily. I grabbed her arms, pulled her into me, and kissed her. She jumped, then fell into my kiss. I displayed the skills I had learned, convincing her physically. My tongue danced with hers greedily, sucking and nibbling and biting. She moaned into my mouth. After a minute, I released her.

"Oh." She gasped as she opened her eyes, transported from another dimension.

"Just... Uh..." I pretended to be nervous. "I mean... We could skip drinks, and you can come over to my place."

"That sounds lovely." She looked at me with hungry eyes. "And Keeya never has to know." She mispronounced her name on purpose.

I turned and walked back to my car, smiling. She didn't know that Kiya would be the first one I told.

"Are you kidding me??" Kiya giggled with glee. "I didn't know you could be so evil." She enunciated the last word seductively. "I'm wet thinking about it, oh my god."

I laughed. "Good, I figured you'd be into it."

"Is Amanda in on it yet?"

"Not yet. I'll tell her when I get to work."

I was so wrapped up in my plan that when I entered Amanda's office, I only then realized my hands were so filthy from the tire. I walked in and paused past the threshold. I stood frozen, my white collared shirt tucked into my gray slacks. My sleeves were still rolled up, exposing my muscled forearms that popped with veins, accenting the black grime collected on my hands, proving the work I had done. When I closed the door, I opened my mouth to apologize and met Amanda's struck gaze. She snapped her fingers to silence me.

"Nope. No. Hush. Lock the door. Right now." She babbled, flushed, and got up from her desk.

I spun to lock the door, and she hurriedly walked towards me when I turned around. I met her in the middle of the office. She took a second to look at me up close. Clearly, she was enamored with my appearance. Suddenly, she dropped to her knees. She reached to my waist and expertly removed my belt, then grasped the front of my pants. She yanked my slacks with an unknown strength I had yet to witness, snapping the button off and shearing the zipper away.

Oh fuck.

She quickly peeled my slacks and underwear down, loosing my cock with one motion. She grabbed it and viciously began orally pleasuring me. I creened my head towards the ceiling, moaning softly; I couldn't tell if this was for my benefit or hers. Her mouth was rapidly and sloppily slurping half of my dick while her hand pumped my shaft. We hadn't finished what we started in the morning, and the surprise and intensity of her attack was forcing me towards the edge.

"Mommy, if you keep going, I'm gonna—" I whispered.

She stopped abruptly, then stood up. Her mouth was wet and salivating, and her eyes were feral and wanting. She pulled on my arm urgently towards the couch, and I walked half steps, my pants still around my knees. As we approached the sofa, she turned me around and shoved me down onto it with surprising force. I scooted back into the cushions, and she stepped onto the couch, her feet straddling my hips, standing above me. I peered up at her. She seemed to be in a divine rage, and her lust consumed her mortal flesh.

I could worship her forever.

She shimmied the dress she wore up her hips and slid her black thong to the side. She squatted down over my lap and grabbed my cock firmly with one hand, then rubbed the tip up and down her slit.

"Oh fuck." I whimpered. I was still sensitive from the morning, and her pussy lips were warm and wet.

She stared me in the eyes while she used me to stimulate her clit, until she finally decided to bless me with herself. She slid my cock to her entrance, let her hand go, and slowly wiggled herself down onto me until my cock was entirely inside her.

"Fuuuuuuuuuuuuuuuck." I groaned softly.

She took her hand that was covered in pussy juice and grabbed my mouth, sealing my lips with her cum covered palm.

"Don't make a sound, baby boy." She ordered.

I nodded slightly, and she bounced up and down my cock gently. I had to fight my urge to moan as I felt her lips grip my cock, the pressure of her walls stretching for me. She squat fucked me with a calm intensity. She was slow and deliberate, clenching her pussy around me at the base as she lifted off, then relaxing as she sat back down. She was milking me, and my cum would be hers soon.

"You need to cum, don't you?" She said in a pouting voice. "You wanna cum in Mommy soooooo bad, don't you baby?"

I nodded helplessly. I felt my cock twitch and pulse, my cum was on the edge. She felt it, and in response, she began going faster and faster. She was expertly stroking my cock inside of her, trying to fuck my cum out of me. I was breathing raggedly through my nose, about to enter my climax, when she pinched my nose closed with her other hand.

I trusted her, but I was surprised I couldn't breathe anymore. She was suffocating me.

"You get to breathe after you cum." She whispered harshly. "Now be a good little boy and fucking cum for me."

I tried taking a breath but was met with nothing but vacuum. My lungs were empty, and the asphyxiation scared me, but the sensation combined with her orgasmic face and her words thrust me over the edge. I erupted with force inside her, my cum exploding into her abyss.

"My dirty little boy is such a slut for me." She whispered heavily. She bounced on me several more times until she slammed her ass down into my lap, quivering and shaking, our mutual climax bonding us forever in that moment.

"Unnggghhhooohhhh. Fuck." She moaned quietly, then released my mouth and nose.

I took a huge breath inwards, feeling lightheaded from the lack of oxygen, and from cumming so hard.

She leaned her forehead against mine and caressed my cheek as she trembled, coming down from her orgasm. "Good boy. MY. Good boy." She cooed.

I was so in love with her. She was everything I could possibly want or need and more. I wanted to stay in that moment forever. She kissed me deeply, and held onto my shoulders as she moved her feet off the couch and rested her knees on either side of me, my half hard cock still inside her. She began grinding slowly into me, my cum seeping out of her and into my lap as she stimulated her clit against me with it.

My cock was so sensitive, but I rode through the pleasure and pain, grabbing her ass with my filthy hands and pulling her deeper onto me. Her movements back and forth got faster and more desperate until suddenly, she whimpered into my mouth as she came a second time. She rode me gently for a minute, moaning, until it passed. When she was done, she broke the kiss and breathed raggedly.

"Thank you, Mommy," I whispered to her.

"For what, baby?" She asked, confused.

"For you," I said simply.

She smiled, then kissed my nose and my forehead tenderly. "I have to get up now, Sweetie."

I nodded, and she carefully lifted off, slid away from me, and quickly ran to her secret bathroom. I sat on the couch in a daze, and after a few minutes, Amanda came back out. She had cleaned herself, put her dress back, and brought a warm washcloth to clean me with. She wiped me down gently and stood me up to pull my pants back into place.

"Oops," Amanda said, her hand covering her mouth. "Looks like you need some new slacks." She giggled.

"Did I—" My breathing was ragged and labored. "Did I really look that good to you?"

She nodded up and down dramatically. "Oh yes." She pondered for a second. "If you had shown up to the interview like that, I would've skipped hiring you and made you my slave instead."

"Sign me up." I grinned wildly.

She giggled, her laugh ringing golden in my ears.

"Now, are you gonna tell me what happened? I didn't give you a chance before." She smiled warmly.

I told her about my eventful morning and the evening I had planned.

She tapped her finger on her lip, thinking. "Devious." She cocked her head to the side, nodding slightly. "Deserved." She grabbed my hands and smiled wickedly. "I'm on board; it'll be fun."

"Before that, though, I need you to ship some paperwork. Gordon has it. While you're out, get a new suit from the tailor." She ordered. "And." She inspected my hands and arms and smiled sadly. "Unfortunately, you do need to clean up."

"Yes, Ma'am." I obeyed.

I got up and used her secret bathroom to wash my arms. I had to scrub four separate times because I didn't want to dirty her towels. Once I was satisfied, I dried off, put my belt back on to secure my pants, and kept my shirt untucked in an attempt to disguise my broken button and zipper. I kissed Amanda and left her office. Gordon was at his desk when I left and gave me a quizzical glance.

"Rough start to the day, eh bud?" Chuckled Gordon when I picked up a large box from his desk.

"Tell me about it." I laughed in response.

I set the box in my passenger seat and made my way to the suit shop. Since the tailor already had my measurements this time, getting a new suit was considerably quicker. I decided I wanted to look extra sharp tonight, so I chose a pitch black suit pinstriped with a slightly lighter black. I also chose a muted pink dress shirt and matching pocket square, with no tie like last time.

After leaving the tailor, I drove to the post office and shipped the package. I realized the part of town I was in was near Miranda's hair salon after seeing my disheveled hair in a window. I needed a cut badly. I made my way to her shop, and this time, the employee at the front was welcoming instead of dismissive.

"Do you have an appointment, Darling?" She asked sweetly.

"No, Ma'am," I responded, shaking my head. "I was hoping Miranda would be able to —" I looked over at Miranda in the back pointedly. "Squeeze me in. Last minute." I played a smile on my lips.

She blushed, nodded, and left me at the counter while she went to Miranda's chair. Miranda was cutting another young man's hair and looked up to me when the employee spoke with her. Her eyes flashed, and she nodded affirmatively. The woman came back to the counter.

"Would you be able to wait about twenty minutes?" She asked, and looked me up and down. "After that, she's all yours."

I smiled. "Of course."

I sat in the lounge area and waited, taking the opportunity to observe Miranda with her customer. She was extraordinarily professional, polite, and didn't flirt a bit —nothing like she was with me.

That means the way she treats me is unique.

The time passed quickly, and soon, the young man walked to the front, paid, and left, looking devilishly handsome. Miranda waved me back, and I strode to her area.

"Hey, beautiful," I said charmingly.

"Did Amanda send you to me?" She asked quizzically.

I shook my head. "I had to get a new suit and figured I needed a touch-up, too."

I stood before her chair, and she moved between me and the mirror. "So you came to me." She trailed her fingers up my chest. "All." She lifted my chin with her hand. "By." She dragged her thumb over my bottom lip.

"Yourself." She lightly pushed my chest, and I fell back into the chair.

I nodded. My dick steeled in response. She looked down at my lap, beaming with joy. She put her hands on my chair's armrests and bent over. Her face got extremely close to mine, and I had a fantastic view of her large breasts.

Good lord. She's just like Amanda but... Different.

"If you're not careful, I *will* fuck you." She stated plainly.

I batted my eyes innocently. "Promise?"

WHAT ARE YOU DOING?

She opened her mouth in surprise. She stood back up and turned around towards the mirror. "You are a bad boy, " she said with mock disapproval.

"Punish me, then," I mumbled under my breath.

WHY ARE YOU ACTING LIKE A BRAT?

Her eyes snapped to mine in the mirror, and she smiled slightly. "I heard that."

I flushed immediately and lowered my head, gazing at my lap. I couldn't help it; she was pulling something out of me that I didn't know existed.

I wish she'd pull something else out of me— Jesus Fucking Christ.

My face was hot with embarrassment, and my dick rock hard. Miranda turned back around with a pair of scissors when I looked up. She started cutting the top of my hair.

"You need to watch your mouth, young man." She said through a smile.

"Make me." I snapped.

WHY.

"Oops," Miranda said, then lunged forward. My head was suddenly buried in her deep, warm cleavage. She had forced her massive breasts into my face on purpose.

Just as quickly, she stood back up and continued cutting my hair like nothing had happened. While she worked on my hair, she frequently lingered her hands on my neck, caressed my ears, and drug her nails down my shoulders. By the end, I was shifting in my seat, my cock very hard and very obvious. I actively creamed precum into my underwear.

She gestured to the mirror. My reflection looked fantastic.

"Wow," I said. "You're incredible," I said, staring at her. I wasn't talking about the hairstyle, and she knew it.

She leaned against her counter in front of me, resting her head in her hand as she peered at me with eyes blue like the turbulent sea. "Were you fucking with me?"

I shook my head slowly. "I don't know why I acted like that; I couldn't help it. I'm sorry."

She smiled softly, her eyes turned to calm waves, and she glanced down at my crotch. "You have nothing to be sorry about."

She reached for a pen and notepad on her counter. She quickly scribbled almost ten items on it. She folded it delicately, began to hand it to me, and then snatched it back before I could take it.

"Give this to Amanda, but no peeking."

I nodded.

What did I get myself into this time?

She handed me the note. I placed it in my pocket, and adjusted my dick with the opportunity.

"Tell her..." She licked her lips. Her face was flushed, her eyes foggy, and I could tell she imagined a scenario with me. "I'm making a formal request."

"Yes, Ma'am," I said without hesitation. Miranda wasn't quite a Mommy like Amanda, but she was still very clearly dominant, and I had reacted instinctively to her.

I stood up and grabbed my suit coat. As I slid my arm by, I slowly and deliberately groped Miranda's ass, and stared at her face while doing so. Her eyes snapped into focus; they sparkled and flamed at my touch. She responded by slipping the palm of her hand down the front of my pants, easing pressure down the length of my shaft.

She leaned over and whispered into my ear. "You really are a bad boy, aren't you?"

All I could do was nod.

I drove back to the office in a daze, wondering what Miranda had in store for me.

I walked into Amanda's office. She looked up from her desk and eyed me up and down.

"Oh, you look stunning!" She exclaimed. "Working hard, or hardly working?"

I gestured down to my semi-tented pants. "You tell me."

"Working hard." She grinned. "Your hair looks immaculate; you went to Miranda?"

I nodded, walked over to her desk, and fished out the note. "She said that she is making a 'formal request.'"

"Oh." She took the note and read it contemplatively. She looked up at me, wary. "Are you okay?"

"What do you mean?"

"I mean, she's a lot to handle and not everyone's type." She said carefully. I knew what she meant.

"I think she's great. She's beautiful and flirty... She doesn't compare to you, but I certainly don't mind her attention." I said honestly. "I acted kind of like a brat with her... I don't know why, but it was really hot, and I think she liked it."

"Really?" She asked, fascinated.

I nodded in confirmation.

"Well, this might be perfect, then." She accepted. "Her and I made a sort of arrangement many years ago. Our fetishes... Overlap, somewhat. If I were ever to find someone like you: submissive, trustworthy, sexy, and—" She rolled her eyes rapidly and blushed. "Just you. I would see if they'd... You'd... Lend yourself to her."

Oh wow. No wonder Miranda didn't flirt with that other guy. I guess I responded to her the right way.

I blushed. "I, uh... I mean, yeah, I'm down." I adjusted myself; blood was pooling into my lap again.

Amanda noticed and smiled. "It'll only be one night. If you satisfy her, she might ask more often, though."

I nodded. "So, what's on the list?"

She looked over it once more. "Preparations. I need to buy some things, and they will take several days to ship, so don't worry about it right now. I'll let you know when we can start."

"Okay." I sighed in relief.

These women are going to fuck me dry.

"Are you still on board with tonight?" I asked.

"Of course, Darling." She leaned forward and caressed my cheek. "Whatever you and Kiya need, I will follow your lead."

"Thank you." I smiled, embracing her hand.

The rest of the work day went by calmly, and we both eagerly awaited the night to follow. We were the first ones out of the office at the end of the day. After we left, I followed Amanda home. She rushed inside and returned with a small box full of the items I knew she had and that I had requested from her. I kissed her on the cheek as thanks, then started towards my apartment. I called Alexis on the way, and she picked up on the first ring.

Oh. Poor girl.

I smiled to myself. "Hey. Are you still coming over? I just got off work."

"Ummm, yes! I'll be right over; send me your address." She replied quickly.

"Well, uh, I need to get home and clean up and stuff." I rambled, feigning a stall for time.

"Don't worry about it, I don't care." I heard her eyes roll over the phone.

"Okay, I'll see you in a minute then." I hung up the phone, set it down, and kept driving.

How long is it gonna take her?

After exactly three minutes, she sent me a text.

'???' She sent.

I laughed. At a stoplight, I responded with my address.

When I got home, I removed my coat, rolled up my sleeves, and moved a wooden dining chair into my bedroom. I set up my stage with the equipment Amanda had lent me, then I sauntered back into the living room and waited. After about ten minutes, I heard a knock at the door.

I opened the door, and Alexis stood there, waiting in leggings and a T-shirt. I stepped aside, and she walked in.

"Hey," I said. "This is my place." I gestured to the room.

"Nice couch, " she said pointedly at the two lawn chairs I had in front of my TV.

Condescending as ever, I see.

I gave a half chuckle. "Yeah."

She raised the six-pack she was holding. "I brought beer for us."

"Good call!"

I walked to the kitchen, and she followed. I pulled a bottle-opening gadget from a drawer and cracked two beers for us. I sat on the counter's edge and pretended to sip my beer nervously.

"Hey, so um." I stuttered. "Well, I know we never did anything too kinky, but there's kind of something I want to try...."

A grin formed on her lips. "Oh really?" She asked, and took a big drink.

I nodded shyly, then set my beer down and moved towards her. She froze; my apparent sudden boldness took her by surprise. I grabbed her hand, set her beer on the counter, and pressed her against my fridge. I locked eyes with her, my lips inches from hers.

"Mark." She gasped. "I like this side of you." She was breathless as I planned: I had stolen it from her.

I kissed her hard, then grabbed her hips and pulled them into mine. She threw her arms around my neck and clung to me, as I reached downwards and squeezed her ass. She moaned into my mouth, then broke the kiss.

"Just fuck me already." She pleaded with a crazed look.

Without hesitation, her fingers found the buttons of my shirt, and she undid the top three before scrambling to pull my shirt over my head. She dragged her nails across my shoulders and down my arms as she admired me shirtless, then her hands found my waist and belt. Before she could unbuckle me, I grabbed her hands and stopped her.

I twirled her around and pulled her ass against my hard cock, while I traveled my hands under her shirt, up her stomach, and palmed her small breasts. She moaned with lust, and I slipped her shirt over her head. She wasn't wearing a bra.

Bet she's not wearing panties, either.

With one hand, I alternated between her nipples, tweaking them. The other hand, I slid between her legs and pressed the fabric of her leggings against her pussy, rubbing it back and forth as she moaned louder. I was correct in my assumption, as the material was wet and slipped and slid back and forth as I rubbed up her slit to her clit. She started bucking her ass against me desperately.

"Just. Fuck. Me." She begged. "Please!"

I didn't answer. I moved my hands from her breasts and crotch, found her hips, hooked my fingers into her leggings, and yanked them down to her ankles. She gasped, bent over, and threw her hands onto the counter, bracing herself. I squatted on the floor and shoved my face into her tiny ass, plunging my tongue into the wet between her legs.

"Oh fuck!" She yelled. "Mark- Ungh—"

I tongued her entrance, and moved my hand around her thigh to thumb her clit. I could tell she was lying about a boyfriend, or an effective one anyway, because she was so touch deprived that my thumb circling her clit nearly caused her to collapse. Making her cum was effortless, and almost instantly her pussy squeezed my tongue, her legs trembled violently, and she started groaning with abandon.

"Uhhhhhhhh- fuuuuuuckk-" She cried as her orgasm swept through her. I heard her voice break as she tried to talk. "Puh- please-

Mm- Marrkk- please-" she sobbed. "Lease- fu- uck- me—" She hiccuped.

I removed my hand and face, then stood up, wrapped my hand around her throat, and pulled her back into me.

"Tha- nk- you—" She stuttered through a weak smile.

"Let's go to the bedroom," I whispered hoarsely into her ear.

She nodded, and then I grabbed her arm and led her to the room. When we entered, she saw I had set up a wooden chair in front of my bed. A large, white vibrating wand was taped to the seat and plugged into the wall. Next to the chair on the floor were several thick leather straps with bright silver buckles. She turned her head to look at me, and her eyes widened.

"Mark—" She uttered fearfully.

I put my finger to my lips and shushed her. She closed her mouth and swallowed. I led her to the chair and sat her down on it naked, with the head of the wand resting in her thigh gap, just touching her clit. I bound her wrists, then her arms beneath the elbow to the wooden armrests of the chair using the leather belts. I used another set to bind her ankles to the legs of the chair. She was immobilized entirely, forced to sit and view the bed. I reached between her legs and switched on the vibrator, and she whimpered softly and bucked her hips against it.

I smiled at her warmly. "Are you comfortable?" I asked, genuinely concerned.

She nodded. "This feels so good." She grinned back lazily, enjoying the sensation on her sensitive clit. "What are you gonna do to me, stud?"

I beamed back at her, amused, and bent over near the chair where a ball gag lay. I motioned for her to open her mouth, and she obeyed. Then, I placed the ball between her teeth and buckled it behind her head. Now, she couldn't speak a sound.

"I'm going to do nothing to you, Alexis." I smiled cruelly.

I turned my back to her, brought out my phone, and texted the girls. Within a minute, she and I heard the front door open. Both Amanda and Kiya walked into the bedroom and saw our state. Alexis's eyes widened in horror. Kiya covered her mouth to giggle, and Amanda gave the bound girl a look full of pity.

I positioned myself directly in Alexis's view. My revenge wouldn't be beating or whipping; she'd probably be into that. It would be neglect. She would watch two gorgeous women, one of whom she feels superior to, pleasure me while she can't do anything.

Without saying a word, Kiya dropped to her knees and unbuckled my pants. Amanda followed suit, and Kiya pulled out my cock with a dramatic gesture.

"It's so big Daddy. Do you think she wants it?" She glared at Alexis while she licked my head lovingly. "Too bad."

Kiya opened her tiny mouth as wide as she could and started sucking me. She took the tip into her mouth and swirled her tongue, savoring my precum, then bobbed up and down, trying to get it deeper. She managed to get about halfway before choking and having to withdraw. Amanda gave her a knowing look.

"Let's give her a show, sweetie." She pulled my dick away from Kiya and bobbed halfway down, then throated me completely. My cock was slipping along her lips, tongue, and the back of her throat as she drooled saliva down my balls.

"Oh my fucking god," I grunted, nearly losing my balance. Her mouth felt incredible, but I knew I needed to do something else or I would cum early. "Fuck. It's too much, Mo- Amanda. Hold on."

Amanda pulled away, grinning like a champion.

I growled at Kiya. "Take everything off."

She looked up at me and started pulling my pants down. I kicked off my shoes and slacks and waited.

She looked at me again, realized, then rushed to rip her shirt and bra off. Afterwards, she stood up, removed her shoes, and peeled down her leggings.

"Stay down there," I told Amanda. She nodded politely.

I sat on the edge of the bed, pulled Kiya onto my lap, and she straddled my hips with her thighs. From Alexis' perspective, all she could see was my knees, Kiya's feet, her ass, her back, and my face over her shoulder. I lifted Kiya's ass off my lap while Amanda moved between my legs and sloppily covered my cock in saliva, then positioned me at Kiya's pussy. I let Kiya's ass down onto me and entered her a third of the way, and she squealed. I lifted her back up, then back down halfway. She grunted, and her head dropped to my shoulder. I lifted her up, then slammed her all the way down onto my cock and she raised her head and screamed to the ceiling. Kiya bounced up and down, roughly, and moaned and yelped with exaggeration.

"Stop," I whispered to her, tilting my head back to meet her eyes.

She pouted.

"This isn't for her. This is for you. Don't fake it." I said.

She huffed, but she settled down. Kiya kissed me softly, her hands pressed against my chest. She slowly moved her hips back and forth, grinding her clit into my pelvis. She squeezed her tight walls around me, and I grunted in pleasure. She smiled into my mouth, happy with herself.

She broke the kiss. "Daddy? Will you punish my pussy?" She asked as she pouted. "Pretty please?"

She threw her arms around my neck, I slipped my arms underneath her legs to get better leverage, and I stood up off the bed. I held her weight in my arms and lifted her off my dick.

I slammed Kiya down onto my cock hard and fast, over and over. I used most of my strength; I wanted her to reach her first orgasm quickly. Soon, I felt her pussy squeeze even tighter than it already was.

"Fuck Daddy oh fuck!" She yelled in my ear. "I'm- I'm- You're making me cuuuummmmm."

After she came, I relaxed a bit and slowly pumped her onto me. I heard a rustling and peeked my head over Kiya's shoulder.

Alexis strained hard and fought desperately to get out of the chair. Unfortunately for her, the leather straps I had used were at least two inches wide, and the chair was an antique: not cheaply made and very stout. She wasn't going anywhere.

If only I had horse blinders or something to immobilize her head to force her to watch.

No, this is cruel enough as it is.

As I bounced Kiya slowly onto me, she started moaning louder and louder. I felt hands on the back of my knees. I realized Amanda had moved backwards when I stood up, but still knelt in front of us, and she must have been using her tongue on Kiya while I fucked her onto me.

"Daddy, her tongue... Oh my gooooddd." Kiya whimpered beautifully into my ear.

"Cum on my dick again while Mommy's tongue fucks your ass," I whispered low in her ear.

Almost instantaneously Kiya's pussy squeezed, she groaned, and I felt cream trickle from her and down my legs.

"Good girl." I praised her.

I slowed to a stop, then turned and deposited her onto the bed. I offered my hand to Amanda, pulled her up, and quickly stripped her of her clothes. When I saw her in all her divine beauty, her cream skin, her ass, her large breasts, I knew I needed to unleash myself upon her.

"Lay down on the edge." I half-ordered and half-asked. She kissed my cheek as a response, then laid on her back with her legs off the bed.

I lifted my arms under her legs and took hold of her wrists. Kiya quickly leant over and slid my cock up and down her soaking pussy, then rubbed it in circles on her clit. Amanda purred with pleasure and anticipation. Kiya put the tip of my cock inside her, and Amanda gasped. I eased inside of her, quickly stretching her and penetrating fully. She moaned as I bottomed out.

"Ohhh fuck. Own my pussy. It's yours baby, make my pussy yours!" She encouraged.

I pulled out almost entirely, then slammed into her and pounded her mercilessly. I was so consumed by fucking her I nearly didn't notice her sounds had become muffled. Kiya had swung her ass over Amanda's face and was riding her, cooing as the older woman ate the younger's pussy. Kiya was facing me, straddling Amanda, with a look of pure heaven on her face. I leaned forward, and she met me in the middle with a deep, longing kiss. As my tongue intertwined with hers, she whimpered into my mouth, and I felt Amanda's pussy contract around my cock as I fucked her. Both women came at the same time, their pleasure penetrating the fabric of the universe.

Kiya and Amanda came together again before I noticed Amanda's enjoyment waning. I motioned for Kiya to get off, and she gingerly, with shaking legs, removed herself. I unlatched my hands from Amanda's wrists and cradled her head, giving her a loving kiss. She kissed me back, then broke it.

"I'm getting sore, Sweetie." She whispered.

I nodded, then looked to Kiya, who had a hungry, expectant face.

"Daddy can you... Can you fuck me like that too?" She asked politely.

I nodded and helped Amanda up and off the bed. Immediately, Kiya positioned herself beneath me with her ass on the edge of the bed. I stood before her with my cock at her entrance and entered her slowly. She moaned deeply as I pressed deeper. I lifted her legs, put my elbows under her knees, and pulled her wrists down beside her ass, pulling her whole body back into me.

"Are you ready, Princess?" I uttered.

She vibrated with joy and nodded. I slammed my entire length into her, and she yelped. I pounded her harder than I ever had before and was rewarded with two screaming orgasms. Amanda climbed onto the bed on her stomach with her head above Kiya's, gazing down at her. I saw her perfect ass and behind it, she shuffled her feet in the air as I thrusted. She whispered to Kiya, guiding her through the intense course. She coached and rewarded the smaller girl every time she came.

"You love Daddy's cock, don't you?"

"You're such a pretty girl."

"You're creaming so much for Daddy."

"You're pretty little pussy is perfect for Daddy's massive cock."

I was running out of steam, but I put the rest of my effort into fucking Kiya. She was breathing deep and rapidly, her pussy flowing cream onto my cock, and her eyes glazed over with satisfaction. I let go of her wrists, put my hands under her ass, and instead of pounding into her, I pulled her body onto me with all of my strength. I fucked her pussy onto me for less than a minute before her biggest climax rushed over her.

"Da- aa- dd- yyy—" She cried and sobbed through the words. "Oh- uh- fuuuuuuuu—" Her eyes closed, her head went limp, and her breathing calmed as she passed out mid-sentence.

I slowed and stopped my relentless fucking. Kiya and Amanda lay on the bed. Kiya was curled into the fetal position, softly snoring. Amanda slowly spread on her back and looked dazed while she stared at the ceiling. She probably couldn't take any more, but I still had yet to cum. I was boiling over.

Give her some kind of reward.

I stood up and looked over to Alexis. She appeared to be vibrating, with rage or pleasure I couldn't tell. I stepped over to her, and my feet splashed against the floor when I approached her. I looked down and saw a puddle had formed in and under her chair.

Oh, I didn't know you could do that.

She glared at me, her eyes emblazoned. I stood before her and stroked myself calmly. I started pumping faster and faster, and felt precum dribble out of me, and it fell to the floor and mixed with her squirt. I stared at her face.

"Do you want it?" I asked teasingly.

If looks could kill, she would be a murderer. But then, she nodded.

"Hmm?" I asked again.

She nodded violently. I smiled. I leaned over, and with my free hand, I placed a finger between her cheek and the leather strap, then tugged downward. The ball gag popped out of her mouth and fell down her chin. I slowly leaned backwards and leisurely took another step towards her. I was enjoying myself. Before I realized, she had thrown her upper body forward, which cut off the circulation in her arms, and flung her head towards my lap. She opened her mouth wide and her lips surrounded the tip of my dick. Surprised, I let go of myself, and she took the opportunity to devour me.

She throated me hungrily, eagerly, recklessly, enveloping my cock in her mouth. She was ferocious, like an inmate on death row, like I was her last meal.

"Oh fuck." I looked down at her. "Fuck I'm gonna cum."

She went back and forth faster as she quivered in her seat. I grabbed her hair and pumped her mouth deep onto me.

"I'm- ugh fuck I'm cumming." I growled as I used her mouth as a toy.

I flooded her throat, forcing her to swallow. She greedily gulped several times as she suffocated on my cock. I looked down and realized her legs were shaking even harder, and I felt more liquid pool off the chair onto my feet and the floor.

I released her hair and pulled my dick from her. She took several massive gasps and nearly passed out. I reached between her legs and switched the vibrator off. She started to settle down and breathe normally. I unbuckled the straps at her wrists and arms, and she rubbed circulation back into her arms while I unbuckled her ankles.

"You okay?" I asked.

She nodded but kept her eyes down and didn't make eye contact with me. I stepped back and leaned on the bed to catch my breath.

You might have overdone it with the humiliation.

Alexis carefully stood up from the chair, her legs wobbling, and she left the bedroom without looking at me or saying a word. I got up and stood at the bedroom door and watched her put her leggings and shirt back on. Then, she walked out the front door without making a sound.

"Hmm," I mumbled to myself. I checked the peephole to ensure she had left, locked the door, and returned to the bed. I laid next to Kiya and Amanda over the covers.

"Was that too much?" Amanda whispered, not wanting to wake Kiya.

I shrugged. "I doubt she'll ask me to fix a tire again."

"Kiya told me something while we were outside waiting."

"What's that?"

"Alexis told Kiya to stay away from you in high school." She said pensively.

"What?" I was surprised that Alexis knew Kiya's name, but I didn't think they had spoken with each other. "Why?"

Amanda shrugged. "All Kiya knows is that Alexis tore into her. Said she would never get to be with you. "

"Hmm." I fell asleep, wondering if Alexis deserved her punishment and if I was justified in punishing her.

Chapter Seven

Amanda and Kiya woke up early the next morning and kissed me goodbye before getting ready for the day. I slept in a little longer, then got out of bed to clean up the mess I made the night before. After I was finished, I checked the time and saw the date.

Oh. Did they forget?

Well, they can't remember if you never told them.

I got into the shower and washed myself quickly. When I left the shower, I saw my phone had a few messages.

They knew!

I opened it and saw they were from Alexis.

'Happy Birthday, loser.' She wrote.

The following message was a picture. She had taken a selfie, her naked body laid seductively on the bed. I could see her from the neck down, and one hand caressed her small nipple. Her stomach was flat and toned, and she was on her side, her hip exposed by the blanket, her thighs crossed, hiding her pussy.

Oh wow. Didn't see that coming.

I walked into Amanda's office, and she was sitting at her desk, beautiful as ever. She looked up and smiled at me warmly.

"Hey, um..." I said hesitantly. "It's... It's my birthday today."

"Oh my god. Baby, I'm so sorry! I didn't know!!" She quickly got up from her chair, moved around the desk, and hugged me deeply. She looked up at me with gorgeous golden brown eyes. "Happy Birthday, Mark. I love you."

"I love you too, Amanda." I bent my head to kiss her passionately. After a minute, I broke the kiss. "It's okay. I only just realized that I never told you or Kiya."

She nodded, released me, and leaned against her desk. "I'm going to take you out to dinner tonight. My treat." She paused and thought for a second. "Is there anything else you want to do to celebrate?"

I shrugged. "Other than dinner with my beautiful beloved? Can't think of a single thing." I smiled.

She blushed, grabbed my hands, and squeezed. "I'll get with Kiya and figure something out."

"Oh shit, I still have to tell her."

She laughed. "Well, go on then, or she's gonna get mad."

She let go of my hands, and I pulled out my phone to call Kiya. She answered on the second ring.

"Baby my pussy huuuurtts I don't think I can get another pounding right now." She whispered in a hushed tone.

I laughed heartily. "No, I was just calling to tell you that today is my birthday. I guess it never came up before now."

"EXCUSE THE FUCK OUTTA ME?!" She yelled. Her voice got quieter, and she apologized to someone. "Sorry... Heh... Mark, what?" She resumed speaking to me. "Why am I only finding out about this today?"

I bared my teeth and looked scared at Amanda. She gave me a sympathetic smile. "Sorry, it's just, y'know, everything's been so crazy, and I forgot."

She huffed. "Okay, I guess Amanda and I will figure out something to do in short notice."

"Nothing too extravagant, please. She's already gonna take me out to dinner."

"Hmm." She paused for a second, thinking. "I think I can work something out for after."

"Alright. I'll see you tonight, then."

"Absolutely. Happy Birthday, Mark!!!" She squealed.

"Thank you, Princess." I smiled, then hung up the phone. I looked at Amanda and breathed a sigh of relief. "That wasn't too bad."

After work, I returned to my apartment to quickly shower and change. I picked a black pair of slacks, brown boots, a brown belt, and a tight black polo shirt that left little to the imagination. I drove to

Amanda's house, and she opened the door in a flowing, sheer black dress. The dress was shorter than knee length, had slits up both thighs, and her breasts spilled out the top. Her eyebrows were sharp under her bangs, and she wore cat-eye makeup. She had stilettos with her cream colored toes peeking out the glossy black material, and her toenails matched.

I grabbed her waist, slid my hands down the dress and felt her ass unrestricted by underwear. My cock greeted her lap when I pulled her into me, and I realized she was slightly taller than me with her heels on. I leaned in to kiss her.

When our lips met, static electricity snapped between us. I recoiled in shock for a moment, then peered into her eyes.

"Let's skip dinner, and you can just..." I paused, breathless. "Own me."

"I'm still sore too, y'know." She giggled. "C'mon. I'm hungry."

I didn't move an inch. I kept my eyes locked with hers. "I am too."

She flashed me a sultry look, then put her hand on my chest. "Later. Promise."

I facetiously pouted acceptingly, resigned that I couldn't have her pussy and eat it too.

I took her hand and led her to the Corvette, opening her door and helping her sit down. I moved over to the driver's side, got in, and made our way to the restaurant.

During the drive, keeping my eyes on the road and not on her was hard. I was hard as well. Her breasts jiggled with every bump and threatened to capsize the vessels holding them. After a thousand glances, I approached the restaurant and exchanged the car with the valet. She led me inside, and we were treated to a luxurious affair. The place was much nicer than the one she had taken Kiya and me to. The floors were black stone, almost like obsidian. The walls and columns were decorated with red velvet plush and golden leaves. I was very much underdressed.

"I don't even own any clothes nice enough for this place," I whispered urgently.

"You are the tastiest snack here," She declared proudly, "by every measure."

I flushed and followed as she stated our reservation to the attendant. We followed them to our table, and I pulled the chair out for her, then sat down. A waiter instantly brought us a tray of fruit.

I spied many of the other patrons looking at us. The men were all older and looked at me haughtily or with amazement. The women were mixed, both young and mature. They either looked at me with desire or at Amanda with envy.

"This is too much." I took her hand across the table.

"Not for you." She said lovingly, then slipped a red piece of fruit past her black lipstick.

"I'm jealous of your appetizer," I said in awe.

She swallowed, then smiled with her mouth open, and the tip of her tongue played between her teeth.

"Settle down, baby boy." She teased. "If you're good, you'll get more than you bargained for."

I nodded, devoting my fate to her caring hands.

After a few minutes, our waitress appeared. She looked about nineteen and wore a crisp white button-down shirt tucked into extremely revealing black slacks. Her hair was pitch black, straight, and covered one of her blue eyes. She took Amanda's order curtly but took my order like she was catering to a king. When she left, she purposefully dropped her pen, bent over slowly, and effectively displayed her shapely, round, delectable ass. I looked a little too long, and I almost thought I could see the seam of her pants split her pussy lips down the middle.

When I looked back to Amanda, she rolled her eyes. "I can't take you anywhere." She said.

"I don't know why," I said weakly.

"Because you're a magnet."

I looked at her quizzically.

"Every girl that meets you wants a taste." She explained. "Or, if they don't want a taste, they at least imagine what it tastes like." She said sweetly and glanced below the table.

The waitress came back with our order, and we ate lavishly. After fantastic food and conversation, the girl brought me the check and winked as she left it with me. I pulled out my card and set it on the tray, got up, and kissed Amanda on the cheek.

"I'm gonna use the restroom before we go."

Relieving myself was difficult as I thought about my date, but I powered through. When I returned to the table, the check was gone, and Amanda seemed annoyed.

"You okay?" I asked, worried.

She smiled at me with a territorial expression. "Yes. Someone was just a little too bold."

"Who?"

She flicked her thumb, and on it was a small sticky note with a phone number. "The waitress pinned this under the check and thought I wouldn't see." She revealed. "Clever, but not clever enough."

I walked around behind her chair and moved it as she stood up. She pointedly crumpled the note, left it on the table, and then handed me back my card. "You make good money now, but not this good."

She paid for it.

"Thank you, Mommy."

"You're welcome, baby." She grabbed my hand as we walked towards the exit. "Disrespectful girls don't get a piece of you." She said plainly. "And I—" She looked at me sharply. "Am your only Goth Mommy."

I nodded quickly.

Noted.

I opened the restaurant door for her and held her soft hand as we walked out. I brought her fingers to my lips as we moved past the threshold. I pulled her close as we stood at the entrance, our eyes locked.

"Have you ever thought..." I hesitated. "About remarrying?" My heart raced.

She could have anyone in the entire universe.

She is the universe.

Her eyes flickered, her face wistful. "Not until recently." She said succinctly.

I wanted to smile, but I pulled her face in my hand and kissed her. "Back to your place?" I asked after our lips parted.

She nodded.

As we waited for the valet, our hands swung in the air like we were grade school sweethearts.

We were driving back to Amanda's house when I told her about Alexis.

"Really?" she asked, and I handed her my phone. "Huh," she said, looking at the picture.

"What?"

She put my phone back down. "Poor girl. She was threatened."

"Threatened by what?"

"By Kiya. In school." She said, looking at me.

"That doesn't make any sense," I replied, confused. "I mean, Alexis was popular. Head cheerleader, rich daddy, drove a lifted Jeep, the whole shebang." I shook my head. "Kiya was poor just like me. She wasn't popular; she was a loner."

Amanda nodded slowly and waited for me to realize.

"So if the loner took the 'it' girl's boyfriend..."

"She'd be ruined," Amanda concluded. "After last night, she realized what she could've had. What she took for granted."

"I uh... I don't feel good about last night." I looked at her with guilt. "I know you weren't very into it either."

She rubbed my arm. "Revenge doesn't taste as sweet as you thought, huh?"

I shook my head. "No, it tastes—" I opened my mouth and squished my tongue a few times. "Like cabbage, actually. Weird." I gave her a dumb grin.

Amanda's laugh filled my soul.

When we arrived at the house, Kiya eagerly waited for us. "HAPPY BIRTHDAY!!" she bellowed as I exited the car and ran into my arms for a big hug.

"Thank you, Princess." I beamed at her. She hopped up and down.

"Come oooooonnnn." She started pulling my hand towards the front door. "Let's get you drunk."

I looked at Amanda, and she smiled; then we all walked into the house.

Amanda had a few steaks in the fridge, and the girls had a blast watching me cook them up and drink whiskey from a glass, shirtless.

After dinner, we lounged on the couch, and Kiya got Amanda's attention.

"Are you ready, Miss Amanda?" She asked excitedly.

Amanda nodded, then rested her hand on my thigh. "Are you having fun, baby?"

"Of course," I said, eying them with suspicion. "What else do you have planned?"

Amanda pulled my face to focus on her. "Do you trust me?"

"Yes," I whispered breathlessly, without hesitation.

"Here." She handed me two small pills, one white and one blue. "Take these."

I looked at them in the palm of my hand. After a second, I threw them onto my tongue, reached for a glass of water, and swallowed.

"Alright." I grinned faintly. "Now what?"

Amanda and Kiya sandwiched me on the couch, their hands rested on and rubbed my thighs. "Now we wait." Amanda purred.

We all talked about nothing and everything for ten minutes. As time went on, I got drowsy, but also felt my cock get harder and harder. The two women kissed my neck and groped my painfully hard cock as I lost consciousness.

I woke up on the couch, groggy and disoriented. I looked down to see my pants were gone, and my cock looked massive; it was nearly purple. It was huge, veiny, and looked almost an inch longer and thicker. Amanda lounged beside me, softly snoring. In front of the couch, four naked girls were cuddled together on the plush floor rug.

Holy shit.

They ran a train on me.

I looked down at my cock again. It was discharging precum, flowing semen every time it twitched.

I need to cum. Bad.

I looked at Amanda, grabbed her leg, and gently shook her awake. "Babe. Amanda. What's going on?"

She slowly stirred and mumbled. "Mmm. Good morning, handsome."

"What happened?"

"We wanted to surprise you, but it didn't exactly go as planned." She whispered, and gingerly sat up.

"The surprise was... Them?" I gestured to the heap of girls.

She nodded. "I gave you a sleeping pill and a viagra. After you fell asleep, Kiya's friends from the basketball team came and..." She paused, staring at my cock. "Had as much as they could handle."

I looked at the girls and realized it was Sheena, Lin, and Mindy. Kiya was down there, too, cuddling amongst them.

"Apparently, they have been pestering Kiya about you for a while. She and I are still quite sore, so this seemed like the best birthday present we could offer." She reached over and stroked my arm. "How do you feel?"

My head was still foggy, but my senses were returning quickly. "I need to fucking cum." I looked at her expectantly.

"The girls all took turns with you, and they spent—" She cocked her head in thought. "Hours. Trying to make you cum. Once their pussies had enough, they all used their hands and mouths..." She smiled as she remembered. "It's rather impressive you didn't cum. Any other man wouldn't have lasted thirty minutes."

Well fuck. If I couldn't cum from that, now what do I do?

I looked at my dick, then at Amanda with a panicked expression. She raised her hand to my cheek and caressed it.

"It's okay, Darling." She settled me. "Don't worry about it. I have a plan to fix it; I was just waiting for you to wake up."

I nodded slowly at her. Her thumb rubbed my jaw.

"I'm going to run to the bedroom and get myself ready real quick. You go ahead and use the girls to get yourself as close as possible."

"Use them?"

"Yes, Sweetie. We all fell asleep waiting for you to wake up. Kiya is out of commission, but the other three can still take a pounding. They want it, I promise." She reassured me.

I nodded. "Okay. I'll get as close as I can."

Amanda nodded in confirmation, and I helped her get off the couch. She sauntered to her bedroom, swaying her hips and ass while she looked back at me.

I stood up off the couch and walked towards the pile of girls. One was face down on the rug, so I knelt at her feet.

Looks like Sheena is first.

I grabbed her hips, and used my whole force to yank her shapely black ass towards me. She grumbled as her knees folded under her. I spread her cheeks and spit on her asshole, then rubbed my cock head in it, down her slit, then back up between her lips at her entrance.

"Fuu.. Uh... Kiya... ?" Sheena mumbled, still half asleep.

I pressed my tip inside her, and she moaned heavily.

"Fuu- uuu- uuu- uuuck."

I pushed and pushed until I my hips met her ass, and I saw a ring of cream collect on the base of my cock.

"Uh... Uh- Mark? Oh fuck." She moaned, waking further as my cock pulsed precum inside her.

I pulled halfway out then back in, fucked her gently, and watched her ass jiggle with every stroke. Lin laid on her side next to Sheena and began to stir after hearing her friend.

"Sheena? You okay?" Lin asked, groggy.

"Mmm. Hmm." Sheena mumbled, and she began shoving her ass back into me.

Lin moved and saw what was happening. "Oh fuck, he's awake." She said, half scared and half excited. "Am I next?"

Sheena nodded, and Lin gulped. "Okay. Um... Will you... Will you... Get me ready?"

Sheena nodded again, unable to speak as I pounded her, and she pounded me back.

Lin grinned, then quickly positioned herself on her back, her pussy in front of Sheena's face. Sheena dove into her and lapped her pussy eagerly. After a few minutes, Sheena began to groan, muffled by Lin, and slammed as hard as she could onto me, cream dripping from her onto the floor. She lifted her head from Lin and gulped for air.

"Enough- enough- I can't—" She gasped between breaths.

Lin smoothed her hair as I removed myself from her. I moved over as Sheena laid herself on her side, and Lin got on all fours and backed her ass towards me. Lin was a very tall, very petite Asian girl, and her ass was small, tight, and firm. Her pussy was dripping wet from Sheena's tongue.

I rubbed my cock underneath, stimulating her clit for a few seconds, before I plunged into her entrance. I got about halfway on the first thrust, and she yelped.

"Oh fuck! Mark- Please- Gentle—!" She yelled.

I slowed my pace and massaged my tip inside her, inching deeper and deeper when I could. After she finally accepted all of me, I grabbed her tiny waist and pumped in and out of her. The consequence of her being so small was that her ass was quite bony, and it hurt my hips when I pounded into her.

"No." I barked. "No doggy. Stand up."

I pulled out, stood up, grabbed Lin's arm, and yanked her to her feet.

"Oh- what—" Lin protested.

I picked her up by her waist, and she shot out her legs and wrapped them around my hips. I reached underneath her and inserted myself back inside her.

"Ohhhhh fuuuuuuuuuccckkk." She moaned as she sat slowly onto me, stretching her once more.

I wrapped my arms underneath her, dangling her knees from my elbows as I held her ass. I thrust upwards, lifted her up, then slammed her back down onto me.

"FUCK! FUCK MARK FUCK—" Lin screamed as I tore her apart.

She wanted 'gentle,' but I can't 'gentle' right now.

I fucked her relentlessly, edging closer and closer to my orgasm while she screamed in pleasure. I slammed her onto me over and over until I felt liquid trickle from her pussy.

"Uuuhh- uhhh- oh god, what is that!?" Lin yelled.

She came with a shuddering climax, and I felt her squirt over my cock and down my legs. She had squirted for the first time. Her arms clung to my shoulders, and her head lolled as her body vibrated violently.

She won't take anymore—next one.

I stopped, knelt to the ground gently, and helped Lin back onto the floor. I looked around and discovered that Kiya and Mindy were awake. Lin's screaming woke them, and Kiya was busy fingering a whimpering

Mindy to prepare her. I knelt on the ground next to Lin and Sheena and pointed to the ground.

"Now," I ordered.

Kiya reassured Mindy, and Mindy crawled on her hands and knees toward me before spinning around. Mindy sat on her knees and bent her chest down to the floor. She kept her knees together, making her tiny ass into a perfect little heart. She was the most petite girl there, even smaller than Kiya. My cock was wet from Lin's pussy, and I slid the tip into Mindy's entrance.

"Oh!" She gasped as I entered her.

Kiya roused Lin and Sheena, and they sat up, unsteady. They saw me and the tiny black girl, looked at each other, then knelt on either side of Mindy, their hands grasping her hips. They put gentle pressure on her, forced her towards me, and she wiggled adorably until she finally took all of my cock with a cute little gasp.

"Oh! Uh- It's- how did you two- uhhh is it even bigger now!?" She whimpered.

I moved my hands over her ass, and as I squeezed it my thumbs slipped down to either side of her pussy lips, engorging and spreading them as I pumped in and out of her. Her pussy left white streaks of cream on my dick as I massaged and stretched her walls.

Kiya got up, moved before Mindy, and sat on her knees. She placed the small girl's head in her lap and brushed her hair and face as she moaned incoherently. I stopped moving, as Sheena and Lin took over for me, pushing Mindy's ass onto me and pulling her back, over and over with perfect rhythm. I watched as her pussy lips gripped my cock, not wanting it to leave, then open back up as it was penetrated again. I was entranced with her ass as it gently slapped my thighs, then decided to wet my thumb and massage her anal entrance.

"Oh! Oh!" Mindy gasped as my thumb applied pressure.

I moved my thumb to the side, spit on her ass, then pressed harder with my thumb, and she relaxed slightly.

"Oh! Oh! Oh!" Sheena and Lin sped up the rhythm, and just as my thumb began entering her asshole, Mindy climaxed explosively.

"O- o- o- ohhh- huh- huh- huhhhhhh." Mindy squealed and pressed harder into Kiya's lap after her orgasm passed.

I was getting close, seeing and feeling the tiny girl cum on my cock had sent me to the edge. "I'm so fucking close," I growled.

Amanda's voice snapped me into focus. "Darling."

I looked over at her. She laid on the couch on her back with her legs spread and up, and she gently pulled a large buttplug from her ass with a plop. "Come." She ordered.

I immediately pulled myself from Mindy's pussy and she wailed as it collapsed without my cock inside. I walked over to the couch and crouched, then rested the tip of my dick at her hole.

"I know your kryptonite, Superman." She purred.

"Your ass, Mommy?" I asked.

She shook her head, reached her arm under my leg, and grabbed me. She pulled and I pushed, and I slid gently inside her ass. She was so tight I knew I wouldn't last long.

"Fuck Mommy. Oh fuck it feels so good, oh my god." I whimpered, my head dropped, and I nearly wept with pleasure.

I was so close. My cock was spilling precum inside her, making her ass even more slippery. Inch by inch crept deeper and deeper within. Amanda wrapped her arms around her knees and pulled her knees together against her chest, squishing her breasts in an image I could barely comprehend. Then, she paired her feet together, rested the arches of her feet against my chin, and her black painted toes onto my lips.

"Suck them." She cooed. "Suck my toes while you fuck Mommy's ass."

I parted my lips, and her toes slid past my teeth. In one moment of perfect clarity, her ass wholly engulfed my cock, and I slipped my tongue through her toes as I sucked, my eyes pinched shut.

I exploded. I came with the force of a dormant volcano, destroying everything in its path. My gorgeous woman came as I came, and our orgasms multiplied exponentially with each other. I pumped my sperm deep inside her anal cavity as her toes wiggled in my mouth, and I clamped down onto them to keep from screaming. Her wails pierced the temporary silence, and we touched Heaven, our bodies One.

"Oh my fucking god."

"That's the hottest thing I can even fucking imagine."

"And we got to see it!!!"

I heard the girls' excited whispers as Amanda's feet left my mouth, her legs opened, and I let myself fall, my face cushioned by her breasts as I lost consciousness once more.

Chapter Eight

I woke up in the morning and learned that after I passed out, not only did Amanda release more cum from her ass than all the girls had ever seen, but it also took every single one of them to help carry me into bed. After Kiya's friends took showers and left, Kiya slept over with Amanda and I.

I stumbled out of bed and took a long shower. I was still a little woozy from the sleeping pill, so I stood in the hot water and let the steam clear my lungs and mind. When I got out, I wrapped a towel loosely around my waist and entered the bedroom. The girls weren't there.

I walked into the kitchen area after I heard them giggling and making noise. When I walked in, they both turned and looked me up and down.

Amanda was wearing her black pajama shirt and matching shorts; her breasts threatened to pop the shirt buttons loose. Kiya wore the same, but it fit bigger, and hers was pink. Seeing both of them instantly made me hard.

Kiya smiled broadly and looked at Amanda. "See! I knew it."

Amanda grinned. "Go on, then."

Kiya walked to me and dropped to her knees. She touched the towel at the fold, and it fell, exposing me in front of her face. She grabbed my cock and lovingly slurped it, wetting it while she gently stroked back and forth.

Amanda came up behind Kiya, pressing her pelvis into the younger girl's head. Her lap pushed her mouth further onto my cock. Amanda grabbed my hands and placed them on her breasts, then kissed me as I fondled them. She thrust her hips back and forth, and Kiya placed her hands on the back of my thighs, throating me deeper and deeper. Her throat was tingly and felt terrific.

She must've used a throat-numbing spray.

I couldn't last more than a few minutes. I moaned into Amanda's mouth, squeezed her breasts, and she forced her hips forward, making Kiya deepthroat me completely. I gushed cum straight into her stomach with a gasp, and Amanda quickly released her so she wouldn't choke.

Kiya swallowed quickly, then eagerly cleaned my cock with her tongue. "Was that good, Daddy?"

"That was." I exhaled. "Fucking. Amazing."

After our mini-session, I put my towel back on and helped the girls cook breakfast. We ate together at the table, and they told me more details about the previous night.

"So it was actually Mindy's birthday, too. We were gonna have the two of you be each other's birthday present!"

"So why did I get a sleeping pill?" I was confused.

"Well... Mindy is really shy. She kind of... She really wanted you but had a panic attack about actually doing it."

"What? Why?"

Kiya shrugged. "She freaks out about stuff sometimes and spirals. She thinks you're really pretty and couldn't handle the thought of you giving your absolute attention to her. It was too much." She explained. "So, we thought maybe if you were asleep, she wouldn't be so nervous with you." She looked embarrassed. "I didn't know if you would... Get hard while asleep, so we gave you a viagra, too. Just in case."

"What about the other girls?"

"When I told them, they wanted to watch. They saw Mindy cum so many times." Kiya grinned. "Sheena and Lin couldn't keep themselves from hopping on for a ride."

Amanda rubbed Kiya's arm. "Turned out to be a little overkill, huh?"

"That's an understatement. Sheena wants another round, Lin can barely walk, and I think Mindy is in love with you now." Kiya said.

"Oops." I grinned.

I needed to go back home and change for work, so I headed out soon after. On my way back home, Alexis called me. After a few rings, I answered.

"Hey," I said tentatively.

"Hello? Why are you ignoring me?" She asked sharply.

"I'm not ignoring you." I lied badly.

"Yes, you are." She snapped. "I sent you a nude on your birthday, and I was planning on sending you more, but you never replied."

"I'm sorry, I—" I paused. "I felt guilty. About what I did."

She was silent.

"Sorry. It was cruel."

"I've been cruel too." She muttered.

"Yeah, but—" I tried to say.

"I get why you did it." She whispered.

"Still."

"Maybe you can..." She clicked her tongue. "Make it up to me."

I shook my head in disbelief. "Do you know why the breakup fucked with me so bad?"

"Why?" She asked quietly, after her flirting didn't work.

"Because not only did I lose my girlfriend, I lost my only friend. My best friend. You were the only one that knew- I mean, you came over that day, after—" My voice faltered.

"Your dad." She said sadly. "I know, I- I don't have any friends either."

"What? You were friends with everyone."

"That was high school, Mark. None of that was real." She fell silent for a time. "I should've just let you be with Kiya." She muttered.

She said her name right this time.

"Do you remember that time in Freshman year, we were hanging out after school, and you were sitting on the ground. I leaned over you, trying to get you to stand up so you would walk with me." She recollected. "Why wouldn't you get up and walk with me?" She seemed sad.

"Oh. Yeah. I remember that." I grinned. "I couldn't get up because I could see down your shirt, and I had a giant, massive boner."

She laughed beautifully.

It's been a long time since I heard her laugh.

"Look, let's actually hang out sometime. Even though you're friend-zoning me—" she said, annoyed. I do... I do miss being your friend." She finished sincerely.

"Yeah, we should. I have to make sure it's okay with the girls, though." I warned.

"Okay, who was the other lady?" She questioned.

"Amanda. She's... Kind of... My boss." I confessed.

Alexis sighed deeply. "That's so hot. I hope I turn out like her one day."

I laughed, and we hung up the phone.

Forgive, but never forget, eh?

I returned to my apartment, changed for work, and headed to the office. When I walked in through Amanda's door, I saw a bunch of supplement bottles all over her desk. I walked over and started reading them.

"L-Arginine, Lecithin, Zinc, Pygeum, Maca Root, Ashwaganda, and Tongat Ali... What is all this?" I asked, puzzled.

"These—" She gestured to the pill bottles. "Will make you cum like a racehorse."

"Wha—" My mouth hung open. "But I already cum so much."

"I've told Miranda how much you produce, but she wants more." Amanda smiled sheepishly. "These increase your testosterone and increase the amount of sperm and ejaculate you can produce."

So Miranda has a cum fetish. Huh.

"So... I just take all these, then see Miranda?" I reached for a bottle. "Easy enough."

Amanda shook her head slowly. "To get the desired effect she wants... You have to take multiple doses of all of these daily. For a week straight." She paused and grimaced at me. "Starting now, you're not allowed to cum until you see her."

My mind went blank. "What??" I was blown away. "How am I... We've been fucking non-stop, now I have to quit?" I complained. "How am I gonna do this?"

Amanda snapped her fingers. "Save the bratty shit for Miranda."

"Yes, Ma'am." I cooled off immediately.

"Kiya and I are both... Acclimating to you. It will be good for us to have a break for a while." She explained. "But, ultimately, it's up to you."

I looked at her in surprise. "No, it's not."

"What do you mean?"

"It's up to you, Mommy," I said truthfully.

She smiled warmly. "I think you'll like it, baby. The waiting will be good for you, too."

I nodded. Amanda had purchased a multi-dose pill box, and we divided all the supplements into seven days.

Seven whole days. Oof.

The first three days passed slowly, but I didn't notice much difference. Amanda had told Kiya about the arrangement, and she was understandably bummed, but went along with it since she thought it would be funny that I couldn't cum for so long. I went through my days as usual, working with Amanda and sleeping on her couch so I wasn't tempted. I didn't see Kiya until the fourth day, which was when my torment really began.

When Kiya and I met at the gym, I was annoyed that I had forgotten my preworkout and shaker bottle, being so full of cum I couldn't think straight.

"Here, have some of mine. Just do a dry scoop." She handed me the tub.

I unscrewed it and got a scoop full. "Can you get me some water for after I take it?"

She nodded, holding up her water bottle.

I leaned my head back and dumped the pre-workout into my mouth. Before I could realize it, Kiya had taken a giant swig of water, stood on top of a bench over me, and spit all the water into my mouth. As I swallowed, my cock started growing.

"God dammit," I snarled, knowing I wasn't able to do what I wanted to her.

She giggled and walked away, swinging her ass in those nearly see-through green shorts.

By the fifth day, time felt like it had slowed to a crawl. I was in agony, and my balls were extremely sensitive. Any sudden motion would cause me pain, so I had to take great care when I sat down, along with slowing my walking pace.

Day six was interesting. I had to bring extra pairs of underwear to work because I would seep precum at such an alarming volume that my underwear was ruined after a few hours. I had a permanent half-erection, but thankfully, Amanda and Kiya were merciful, both abstaining as much as possible from my presence.

At the end of work on the seventh day, Amanda gave me a sweet kiss on the lips, wished me luck, and sent me to Miranda's house.

I arrived at Miranda's house, nervous, aching, and horny. Her place was a large, two-story, modern style, and she answered the door after several knocks.

"Took you long enough," I said, and rolled my eyes when she opened the door.

She smirked. "Are you ready?"

I looked at her expressionless. "If blue balls are fatal, I will perish in thirty seconds."

"Ohhh. Poor baby." She said, facetiously concerned.

"Feed me, then." I snapped.

"Hah! Come in, silly." She moved from the door.

I walked inside. It was even more impressive than the architecture exposed to the world. It was full of plants, stone, and exposed beams. She could be an interior designer.

"How did you afford all this?" I asked, amazed.

"I do own the hair salon, after all." She stated.

I was floored. "But you... You nearly stripped me down when you cut my hair."

She grinned. "My employees were certainly surprised, to be sure."

I was embarrassed and fell silent.

"Don't worry about it." She moved towards me, touched my chest, and started unbuttoning my shirt. Her hands on me made my cock respond instantly.

She draped my shirt off my shoulders, then unbuckled my pants slowly. Just before unbuttoning my pants, she stopped abruptly, breathed in sharply, then exhaled. "I haven't eaten all day waiting for this."

I was vibrating. My dick was wearing a hole through my pants trying to get to her.

She took her hands away. "I don't want to get ahead of myself."

I huffed.

She glared at me. "Do you want to cum or not?"

I nodded.

"Hmm?"

"P- p- please." I pleaded. My knees were weak. "I'll b-beg if you want me to."

She smiled. "That won't be necessary." She gestured up and down at me. "Naked." She pointed down the hallway. "The room down to the left."

I nodded. As she walked away, I pulled off my shoes, stripped my clothes, and left them in a heap on the floor. I entered the room and found it empty except for several pillows and a blanket underneath a large table cushioned with black leather. I inspected the table, finding a small black strap with a buckle on it and an interesting hole in the middle of the table.

Miranda walked in behind me. She wore nothing but red panties and a massive red bra holding her breasts. My breath was stolen by her. She stared at my cock, erect, dripping, and nearly purple. She smiled and licked her lips.

"That strap. Put it on." She ordered.

"Where?" I asked, the single word lingering with brattiness.

"Where do you think? Its purpose is to keep you from fully ejaculating."

"Oh." I grabbed the strap, and secured it under my balls and around my cock and buckled it. I didn't tighten it completely, just enough to apply some pressure.

"Let's get you started." Miranda snatched a pillow from under the table and knelt on it in front of me. She pulled me towards her and delicately licked my cock head, tasting the juices already leaking.

She swished her saliva in her mouth, and poured it down between her breasts, then folded my cock underneath the front strap of her bra and between her breasts. She kept drooling on it, dribbling spit down onto my cock as she moved her tits up and down, squeezing them together.

"Oh fuck. Oh fuck. Fuck fuck I- I- I'm—" I was so deprived that the incredible sight and feeling of Miranda's heavenly hosts was sending me over the edge.

"Not yet." She expertly removed my cock in seconds, and placed her thumb at the base of my cock, putting pressure on my urethra. I clenched and held my breath, knowing I was going to explode anyway.

"Push!"

What? Oh, like Amanda made me.

I took a deep breath and pushed as I exhaled, and slowly the sensation of having to orgasm turned into gently flowing sperm through my cock. She slowly released her thumb and caught the wave of precum I poured in her mouth.

She tasted it like a fine wine and swallowed. "Oh, Mark. You really did wait the full week, didn't you?"

I nodded, breathless and wobbly.

She beamed at me. She stood up and motioned me towards the table. "Lay face down, and put your package through the hole."

I nodded and did as she ordered. Once I was on the table, I pressed my face into a U shaped headrest, and closed my eyes, enjoying the sensation of my cock and balls hanging in space. After some rustling underneath me, I felt Miranda's lips on my cock, and her hand gently massaging my balls.

The sensation was indeed something to behold. Over the course of an hour, she teased me, bringing me to the precipice of orgasm over ten times, each time making me push and gush pre-ejaculate into her welcoming, greedy mouth. By the eighth time, I was freely weeping tears from my eyes. By the tenth, I was sobbing.

"Please," I begged, debasing myself. "Please oh my god, I can't- I- It feels so good it fucking hurts, I'm so sensitive!"

"Hmm." I heard her muffled under the table. "This is by far the most cum I've ever had in one sitting. I'm practically full. I guess... I could..."

"PLEASE, MIRANDA!" I screamed.

She throated me, grabbing my balls and squeezing gently. She bobbed down and up, milking my cock, then, using the release snap on the strap, took off the leather restraint. I felt blood rush down into my cock, and the tip of me inside her throat sent me spiraling.

"UUGGHHG FUUUUUCK." I bellowed, emptying seven days of cum down her throat.

Miranda swallowed and swallowed a second time, then began choking as my cum overflowed up her throat, along my cock, and out past her lips. She held me in her throat, pulsing as I gushed cum down her neck and breasts.

I had to focus on breathing to keep from passing out. After it was evident I had released everything I had pent up, she let my cock slide out of her mouth. She left the underside of the table and stood in front of me. I looked up, exhausted, to see her voluptuous figure, her red-clad breasts bathed in my semen.

Miranda was speechless. "That was... So much..." She was in a daze. I had given her a throat creampie. She lazily used her hands to mop up my cum, bringing it to her mouth and drinking it as she cleaned herself. "No wonder Amanda likes you." She said, astonished.

"Did- Did I- Was it enough for you?" I asked, worn and weary.

She nodded approvingly. "Yes. More than enough." She paused. "But I will need more."

I looked at her, terrified.

"Once you recover, of course." She smiled.

I breathed a sigh of relief.

Miranda sat me naked on her couch and gave me a glass of orange juice and a peanut butter and jelly sandwich.

"Act like a brat, you get brat food." She teased.

"I'm not complaining one bit." I downed the orange juice in two swallows and got to work on the sandwich. I was starving after being milked dry. Miranda had fetched a plush pink bathrobe and sat on the couch next to me.

"How much do you know about Amanda's divorce?" Miranda asked curiously.

"I know they couldn't have kids, which caused it." I finished the sandwich. "The subject made her uncomfortable, so I haven't pried."

Miranda nodded slowly. "I think you need to hear the whole story before you do what I know you're planning to do."

"How do you know?" I swallowed.

"I'm smarter than you." She grinned.

"Oh." I looked down. "So... What happened?"

"Amanda was married at your age. They were high school sweethearts." I nodded. I knew that much. "After a few years, she started at the company. Did what you do. They tried for a kid... And she miscarried."

I nodded somberly.

Miranda's gaze was a laser in my eyes. "After she miscarried, he beat her so savagely that she... It's impossible to—" Her voice cracked, and her eyes welled with tears. "She will never have children."

"What?" My voice was hoarse, and I was horrified.

"She had to get surgery, and..." Tears flowed from her eyes. She wiped them with her fingers. "We were already close friends then. I made her live with me while the court proceedings dragged on. The divorce and protective order... It was a rough few years."

I put my head in my hands. "I know what it's like to be beaten savagely," I whispered.

"Oh, Sweetie." She rubbed my arm. "We've all got something. The two of you just seem to match your something's well. Hell, I haven't seen her like this with a man since... Ever."

"Why me?"

"Who wouldn't love a big strong man doting on you?" She asked, grinning. "But really, deeper than that: you're vulnerable."

Huh?

She could see my confusion. "Look, Mark. How is a woman—especially a woman who has been through hell like Amanda—how is she supposed to trust a man who can't be vulnerable? Most men can't be vulnerable with a woman. So they hide behind a facade because they refuse to appear weak." She leaned back. "But you..." She snapped her fingers. "Everything on the table, immediately. You offered yourself; you put yourself into her hands. That's exactly what she needed."

That's why she was so quick to claim me—it was her ownership ritual. It was a claim, but it was also protection.

"She's exactly what I needed, too," I whispered.

"So? Are you gonna do it, or what?" She asked.

"Yeah."

I drove back home to Amanda's house. We talked about the sex, and we talked about her ex. We talked about my parents, too.

Violence and neglect... And regret. They're all things we both share. Somehow, someway... We're supposed to be here.

I fell asleep in her arms, in her breasts, and slept well. Soundly, thoroughly, and safely. Invincible, because I was with Her.

When I woke up in the morning, I heard the shower running. Then I heard Amanda singing beautifully in a high key. She could sing in an angels' choir.

"For so long, I have waited
So long that I almost became
Just a stoic statue, fit for nobody
And
I don't wanna get in your way
But I finally think I can say
That the vicious cycle is over
The moment you smiled at me"
"And just like the Rain..."

She trailed off as she washed herself.

I know that song.

I got out of bed, walked into the kitchen, and decided to make her eggs for breakfast. I sang the part of the song that I knew in a deep baritone, naked, with only a half apron on as I cooked for her.

"I know, I know, the way that it goes
You get what you give, you reap what you sow
And
I can see you in my Fate.

I know, I know, I am what I am
The mouth of the wolf, the eyes of the lamb
So darling will you saturate?"
"And just like the Rain
You cast the dust into nothing
And wash out the salt from my hands
So touch me again
I feel my shadow dissolving
Will you cleanse me with pleasure?"

I finished the eggs and plated them. Amanda had finished her shower and walked into the kitchen to listen.

"Nobody can say for certain
If maybe it's all just a game
When I open my eyes to the future
I can hear you say my
Name."

She wrapped her arms around me, and we sang together.

"So Rain down on me
Ohhhhh Rain down on me"

She giggled. "You know that song is about squirting, right?"

I embraced her embracing me. "Ohhh. Yeah, that makes so much sense."

We sat at the table and ate, enjoying our serene moment of peace.

I had to take my car back to my apartment to change. When I entered, I took a moment and looked around.

I don't really spend any time here anymore.

I showered quickly and got ready for work, excited about the plan I was forming. I just had to make it through the work day before I could put it into action.

The morning was slow but wonderful, as I didn't have to refrain from physical affection with Amanda anymore. I kissed and held her, longer than necessary, just to feel her. She took the opportunity to tease

AMANDA'S MARK 141

me as well, licking her lips and grabbing a handful when she could. After lunchtime passed, Amanda needed me to copy a document.

Gordon approached me when I left Amanda's office. "Hey, bud, can I talk to you for a second?" He saw my face and reassured me. "You're not in trouble." He laughed.

"Sure! Can you walk?"

"'Course!" We walked together to the copy room.

"I realize no one is supposed to know, but I'm sure you're aware that you and Amanda are the office's open secret." He started.

I looked around as we walked. "We are?" I said in a hushed tone.

Gordon chuckled. "Yes, y'all are." I opened the copy room door for him, and we went inside.

"Y'know, Amanda and I started working here together all those years ago." He said when the door closed. "We were great coworkers and better friends. Then, after her divorce... She changed. She wanted everything; she wanted to be at the top. I wasn't going to get in her way, so I helped her when I could. But, she changed. She wasn't happy, not anymore."

Gordon paused for a moment. I didn't speak. I knew that sometimes, older men would divulge truly personal things if you didn't interrupt and let them think and speak.

He cleared his throat after a long minute of reflection. "I think... I think when someone works their fingers to the bone to get to the top, to have everything... But they don't have anybody... They realize that they really have nothing at all."

He put his hand on my shoulder. "Mark, after you got hired, I noticed a change in Amanda. Now I see it more than ever." He gazed at me with watering eyes. "I don't know what you did, but you gave me my friend back. You're... You... She's the real Amanda, again. She's happy. I just want you to know how much that means to me."

I shook Gordon's hand and pulled him in for a half hug. "Thank you for telling me that, Gordon. I appreciate it."

Alright, that's it. Can't wait any longer.

After my talk with Gordon, I returned to Amanda with the copy.

"Hey, I need to take a half day," I said.

"Is everything okay?" She asked, concerned.

I beamed. "Everything is perfect. I just need to go get something done. Actually, can you pick me up after work? I want to go to dinner, but nothing too fancy."

"Sure baby, go ahead." She smiled.

I walked out of the office, confident in my decision.

Time to figure out how much this car is worth.

Chapter Nine

Amanda picked me up at my apartment. I wore black slacks and a slightly transparent white button-down shirt that accentuated my figure. She wore a gorgeously simple black sundress, and she looked ethereal. She brought me downtown to a quaint restaurant I could afford but had never seen before.

"It's a little hole-in-the-wall. The food is so good, though." Amanda said eagerly when we walked in.

"I hear Mexican music coming from the kitchen." I nodded approvingly. "I already know this is gonna be good."

Our drinks were served in blue and red plastic cups, and it was nice to share something with Amanda that wasn't luxury, something I could relate to. I certainly appreciated everything she provided for me, but knowing that we were just as content eating together at a greasy spoon as a Michelin star was comforting.

"I missed you," Amanda said and reached her hand over the table.

"I missed you more." I gave her a pointed look. "I had forgotten how intoxicating being near you is."

"Forgotten?" She asked innocently. "Or blocked out, because otherwise you would've..."

Her foot had slipped out of her shoe and moved into my lap, gently rolling and caressing my ever-growing cock.

"Cum?" She said with a sweetness that rivaled the finest confectionery.

I gulped and nodded.

She grinned, removed her foot, and looked around the place. It was a little grimy but had so much character that hygiene was easily overlooked.

"I used to come here when I was your age." She said wistfully. "I haven't been here for so long, and I... I wanted to share this with you."

I took her hand. "Thank you," I said sincerely. "Living in the lap of luxury is nice, but places like these are good for the soul."

She smiled. "Exactly."

We ate our delicious food that rivaled the priciest gourmet at a fraction of the cost. While we ate, my decision was fixed in the back of my mind. I was nervous, and I wanted to wait for the right time. In truth, I was terrified.

Indecision is still a decision.

But I don't even have the ring yet.

Does that matter?

We finished eating, paid and tipped handsomely, and walked outside holding hands. It was a dark night, and we could see a few stars in the sky. We strolled down the sidewalk as we stargazed, only a few blocks from Amanda's car, and I built the courage to ask her the question.

I abruptly became hypervigilant.

As we walked, a man turned a corner and followed us.

"Walk in front of me," I uttered, placing my hands on her hips and positioning her so that I blocked the man's view of Amanda.

"What?" She asked, still not aware of the situation.

The man increased his pace.

"Let's pick it up," I murmured, nudging her forward.

"What's going on?" She whispered as she walked faster.

"He- hey—" I heard the man speak behind us.

Flight isn't working; fight is the next course since you're with Amanda.

My fingers and tongue went numb. In a split second, I felt a tingling surge wash over my neck and down my shoulders; my body had dispersed sweat through every one of my pores. My heart raced, and my breathing shortened to quarter breaths.

"If it goes down, you run." I urgently told her.

"Mar—"

"HEY!" The man yelled. He nearly sprinted as he closed the distance between us.

I stopped and spun in place, extending my arms low to my side in front of Amanda.

"How can I help you?" I stated plainly, my eyes narrowed into a laser focus as I caught his image.

He was about my height, wore filthy flannels and torn jeans, had an unkempt beard, and had scraggly hair. The most crucial detail my eyes noticed was that his left hand was at his side, but his right was positioned behind him.

"I wanted your wallet, but now I want her." He said, raggedly breathing after he had stopped some distance from us.

"The fuck did you just say?" I sliced with derision as my anger welled within, and I stepped towards him.

He whirled his right hand around, which held a pistol, and waved it at me.

"I just want a feel and won't have to shoot you." He sneered as the barrel of the gun drifted to my left, to me, to my right. As he spoke, I moved gently closer, closing the distance so his angle was on me instead of Amanda. "Whatd'ya say, big guy?" He said mockingly.

Well, that's an easy decision, at least.

Two-for-one special, too, if I don't make it.

I acted like I was thinking it over and took a slow, deep breath. The barrel moved from my right side to my center, and just as it went past my center and to the left, I exhaled, lunged forward, and my hands reached for his weapon.

The gun fired, but he missed, yet somehow, when I made contact, he managed to punch me in the chest. The wind was knocked out of me, but I quickly controlled the angle of the gun and glanced back towards Amanda, checking on her.

She was screaming, but my ears rang terribly from the shot, and it didn't seem as though she was hit. I controlled the gun, twisted it in his hand, and it clattered to the concrete. As soon as I heard it, I grappled his neck, forced it down, and cemented him in a front headlock. I squeezed with all my force, and he punched me several times as he struggled. The wrestling I did years ago actually paid off.

His punches feel weaker than the first one.

His hair must have been soaked in sweat because my chest felt like a cup of water had been dumped on it. He slowly struggled less as his body's oxygen supply exhausted, cut off from breathing air.

You're losing strength.

My arms felt weak. They loosened, and he managed to twist away from my grip frantically. He threw my arms away, broke my hold, shoved me backwards, and ran away.

You need to breathe.

I can't.

I tried to breathe in, but my throat gurgled as I inhaled. I had choked on pool water when I was younger, and it was a similar feeling—except the water was warm instead of cold. I felt like I was somehow drowning in dry land. I touched my chest; it was dripping wet.

Warm. Warm and wet.

As I collapsed onto the sidewalk, my hearing transitioned from a deafening ringing to a slow, dull drone. I heard Amanda's muffled screams, and she ran towards me. She dropped to her knees and felt over my chest.

Her hands came back red with blood.

Fuck.

She scrambled to grab her phone from her purse, and I heard her calmly speaking with the operator. After a minute or two, she set the phone down and listened as the operator told her what to do. She placed both hands on my chest and applied pressure.

"Stay with me, Mark. You belong to me, remember?" She pleaded.

I belong to Amanda.

AMANDA'S MARK

We stayed like that for several minutes before I heard a siren. It rapidly approached our location and then cut out. I heard a car door slam and footsteps running towards my head.

"Mark Sampson? What the fuck?"

I looked up to see a large black man in a police uniform.

I rolled my eyes so hard they nearly popped out. "Kanye." I gurgled between quarter breaths. "Of course you became a cop."

"What happened? Who shot you?" He asked.

Amanda spoke. "How do you know, Mark?"

"School bully," I stated simply.

Amanda looked pissed. She barked at Kanye. "He wanted me. Mark stopped him and got shot." She continued to describe the guy and what he was wearing. She nodded towards the direction he went. "Ran that way. Do your job, please."

Kanye relayed the information over the radio to his fellow police officers. He stuttered, replying to Amanda. "Y-yes Ma'am."

Hah! Even Kanye is scared of her.

"Mark, medics are on their way. Told them we cleared the scene, so they'll be here in a minute."

He told his partner who ran up to us to secure the gun, then ran off towards the shooter.

"It'll be okay, baby. They'll be here soon." Amanda whispered, her arms straight as she put her weight into my chest.

I nodded.

I belong to Amanda.

After a minute, I heard a different kind of siren approach and then cut off. I heard doors slamming, and several people came and dropped equipment bags next to me.

"Hey, buddy, what's your name?" A cute man knelt next to my head and grabbed my wrist. A smaller lady knelt next to me and began cutting my shirt off.

"Mark Sampson."

"Okay, Mark, what year is it?"
"2024."
"Who's the president?"
I rolled my eyes.
He chuckled. "Good enough. Is Mickey Mouse a cat or a dog?"
"Neither."
"Fantastic. Alright, Mark, we gotta do a bunch of stuff. Just keep talking to me, okay?"

One of the medics gently moved Amanda aside and opened a package of white fabric.

"After the combat gauze, put a chest seal."

Her fingers dug into the hole in my chest painfully, and I winced with every movement. She was done quickly and placed a square seal on my chest after wiping the blood away.

"Mark, buddy, say something to me." The man ordered.

I opened my mouth to speak but couldn't form a word. I coughed, and blood seeped out of my mouth.

Belong to Amanda.

"Mark, we have to roll you over to check for an exit wound. Then we'll get you into the ambulance. Sound good?"

I struggled to breathe, and my eyes drooped and closed. I felt like I was drowning in a warm bath, slipping into sleep.

"Mark? Mark!"

Belong. Amanda.

I heard Amanda screaming. I felt her hands on my face. Her tears rained down on me.

"MARK, DON'T LEAVE ME! I NEED YOU, DON'T LEAVE ME ALONE!"

Her screams were muffled, as though I heard them through a film of water. My body jerked to the side, back down, and then I was lifted up.

My eyes, adjusted to the darkness, were sensitive to the light of the ambulance, but it slowly faded through my eyelids, and the sudden brightness gradually dissipated into the ether.

Amanda.

"C'mon, buddy. C'mon."

I felt pain in the center of my chest, and I spasmed uncontrollably. Their voices sounded so far away.

"Still responsive to pain— Mark— If you can't wake up—This tube—Throat— Big needle— Chest—"

Amanda.

I felt the pain again, but it was only a trickle of sensation light years beyond.

"Unresponsive to pain."

I was aware of my mouth opening, and something slid past my teeth. I felt another trickle going down my throat. I felt a slight pinch between my ribs. I felt a weight lift off my chest, but if I had been deep under the waves before, I would have been just below the surface, still floating.

Amanda.

"Year old male— GSW—Chest—Through and through, exit wound—Trauma Alert—ecompensating—Intubated— Tension pneumo—Needle Decomp—Five minutes—"

Amanda.

Am.

A.

A.

.

Chapter Ten

I was surrounded by trees, and their canopy bridged through the pitch night sky. There were no stars, only a faint orange glow in the center of a small clearing where I stood. A campfire. A man. He sat, his body blocking my view of the flame, and I could make out his silhouette in the glow.

"Hey," I said. I walked towards him. My feet were bare, and the clothes I had on... nothing. There were no clothes.

This will be awkward.

I cleared my throat as I approached him. "Hey."

No response. I saw him sat on a stump, hunched over the fire. The back of his head was square, his hair short, neat, and flowing. His clothes... He wore a black hoodie and blue jeans—one of my old outfits. I stood directly behind him.

"Hey. I guess I lost my clothes—" I started to say.

"Why did you attempt?" He said, his voice familiar.

"What? What does that even mean?"

His head snapped around to face me, and I saw myself.

"Why did you try to kill yourself?" He asked, almost yelling.

"What the fuck? What is this? Who the fuck—"

He stood and faced me in one movement and shoved me backwards. I stumbled back but caught my footing.

"Why?" He snarled.

"I- I've never- never tried to—" I stuttered, shocked at seeing myself.

"You know exactly what you did. Two-for-one special, right?" He asked.

I froze.

"You get to die, and that worthless fuck gets to rot in prison for murder!" He shouted accusingly. "What about Amanda? Kiya? All the others? Are they not good enough for you? Or are they just Band-Aids for your misery?"

I scoffed.

"Hmm. Pride." He said slyly. "You're fucking pathetic." He spat at me.

"Fuck you!" I yelled at him.

"Ah. Anger. Your righteous anger. So mad at the world, at me, at everyone and everything. You use it to lift. To punish."

"To fuck." He drawled.

I scrunched my face at him.

"How dare the world deal you these cards. HOW DARE THE WORLD MAKE YOU FEEL THIS WAY." He bellowed.

I flinched.

"Your mother saw it." He taunted. "Your mother knew what festered inside you. Not the only thing you inherited from your father. But the most potent. You can't ignore it. You can't hide it from me. She couldn't love you because she knew."

I seethed.

"She could see your soul, and she knew your soul was defective." He whispered.

I snapped my eyes to look at him with hate.

"That's why she hated you, because you are just like your father!" He yelled.

I lunged towards him. I had never hit anyone in my life, yet I planted my foot, twisted my hips, and used all my force and weight to strike my fist into his face. He fell backwards towards the fire, collapsed, and his head hit the stump with a thud. I leapt onto him and straddled him as I kept punching his face.

"Fuck you. Fuck you. I fucking hate you." I hit, hit, hit, over, and over, and over.

He smiled up at me, teeth bloody, red spit dripping out of his mouth. "Do it."

"I'll fucking kill you," I whispered in rage. I wrapped both my hands around his throat and squeezed, feeling his windpipe crush under my strength, and I screamed at him. "I'LL FUCKING KILL—"

My grip loosened, and his throat got smaller. Suddenly, I was strangling my fourteen-year-old self.

"You're gonna kill me? Like Dad tried to?" He whimpered, his voice cracking.

I recoiled and hurled myself back from him and onto the ground. I stared, horrified, at him lying on the ground, then at my bloody and bruised hands. Tears streamed down my face.

"Fuck." I sobbed. "Fuck."

I wept. There was nothing left of me but sadness. I was hollow—a shell.

"There it is. Sorrow." My younger self whispered. He sat up and watched me. "Everything you are ends at this. As all roads lead to Rome, all your roads lead to despair. The misery is you, and you are miserable. Do you think it would cease if you ceased?"

"What?" I croaked.

"If you perish... Like this... All your burden would bear upon your loved ones. Exponentially." He stated it like it was simple. "Do you wish that for them? Do they deserve such a fate? Did they earn the wretchedness that you have so carefully cultivated?"

"No." I shook my head hard. "No. They're not weak but... That's not fair. It's mine. It's mine to carry."

I looked at him, broken and bloody. Me.

"How do I move on? I'm broken. I've always been broken." I asked after several minutes.

"So?"

"What do you mean, so?" I asked, annoyed.

"To be broken is to be human. Are you not human?"

"Of course I'm human," I responded. "I'm supposed to be a man." I professed pathetically.

"What is a man?"

"I don't know," I said in truth. My father was a sad excuse for one. Gordon was a man, I supposed. I didn't have a real example or know what a man should be.

"Does anyone?" He reasoned.

I didn't have an answer.

We sat in solemn silence, and years passed in seconds. I watched him age from fourteen to twenty and beyond. He grew a thick beard, sexy gray streaks through his hair, his face chiseled and handsome, his body muscular and proud. Lines etched his face from worry and laughter. He was everything I could hope to be and more.

"What am I supposed to do? Who am I supposed to be?" I asked, pleaded, and begged my elder self.

"You're supposed to be alive, Mark, simply because you are alive." He smiled. "You're supposed to be yourself, simply because you are you. That's all."

I swallowed the sentiment. I looked at him, and he looked at me. I looked at myself, wondering if I had survived. This place wasn't hell, it wasn't heaven, it wasn't even purgatory. It was just...

Me.

"So... When do we leave this place?" I asked quietly.

He shrugged. "That's not really up to me."

I nodded. I stood up, wiped blood and tears off of my face, and sat down next to the fire.

After gazing into the flames for countless eras, I noticed a different shade of orange that didn't emanate from the fire. I looked up at the sky and saw light peeking through the circle of trees.

"Hmm." He grunted, a faint smile on his lips.

I floated in nothingness. It wasn't black or white. There was no color. I felt nothing. No sensation on my skin, no sight, no smell... I was nothing.

Then I heard a melody.

"Life keeps telling me I need to go
But what if I wanna stay?
'Cause I'm lost here without you
Without you"
"And I need you now 'cause it's killing me
And I wish somehow you were here with me
When I fall asleep, I feel you with me
'Till I fall asleep and you are with me"
"I found a love I never had before
You changed me
And I will wait however long it takes
You changed me
"You say the words that I've been thinking
I'll never let you go"

I pondered. There was nothing else to do. I was nothing except a consciousness and barely that.

I realized the song was about a man waiting for his love. No one would sing that song if they had their love.

Am I waiting for someone? No, I'm nothing.
Then, who is waiting for me?
A?
A.
Am.
Amanda.
AMANDA.

My eyes opened. I stared at an ugly white drop-down ceiling with a fluorescent light bar. I was acutely aware of a large plastic tube in my throat. I tried to breathe but wasn't able to. A machine sounded and whirred; oxygen forcefully filled my lungs and expanded my chest. I reached up to my mouth and grasped the tube. I pulled on it, and it was caught in my throat.

This thing is really in there.

I yanked hard, slid it out of my throat, and nearly vomited. I took a heaving gasp of air, relieved. I stared at the tube, then dropped it beside me. I looked down at my arms. Needles protruded from both of my hands, connected with long transparent tubes filled with liquid and hooked up to bags. The machine to my right started beeping. It had numbers and a yellow CO_2 marker flashing. I squinted and saw a small red button that said 'silence alarms' and raised my arm with considerable effort to press it. The beeping stopped, thankfully.

I looked over to my left. There was a woman, disheveled, in leggings and a black shirt. She was sitting sideways in a chair, her knees to her chest, her arms wrapped around her legs. She was asleep, snoring softly, and her black hair draped haphazardly down her face. Her head rested on top of her knees, her face pointed at the bed I laid in. She had several gray hairs mixed with the black. Her face was sad, pained, wanting. She was gaunt, her cheekbones sunken, her body at least twenty pounds lighter than she should've been.

"Am." I croaked. "Am."

Tears flowed down my face.

"Am. Anda." My voice was raw and sliced my throat as I attempted to speak.

She spasmed slightly like a cat dreaming.

"Am. Anda. Amanda." My throat was a gravel road, and my voice was barefoot in the stones.

"Amanda. Please—"

Her eyes snapped open.

"Mark. Mark!"

She unfolded, leapt out of the chair, and over to my bed.

"Mark—Mark—You're—awake—" She sobbed uncontrollably and spoke with hiccups.

Her face was the most beautiful thing I could even imagine. My heart flooded, and I sobbed with her.

"How- how long—" I choked.

"Five. Five weeks. You've been gone for five weeks." She cried.

"Oh my god. I can't- I'm sorry- I'm so sorry- Are you okay?" I stuttered.

She shook her head violently and awkwardly climbed the rail attached to my bed. She straddled me, dug her arms underneath my chest, and buried her face into my neck. I wrapped my arms around her, greedy for her embrace. We wept. Together.

I'm alive. Amanda's okay.

I'm alive.

I belong to Amanda.

A nurse burst in to find us together. She fetched a doctor, and the doctor asked questions and gave answers. The doctor tried to get Amanda out of my bed, but she wouldn't listen. I scooted over to the other rail, and she laid beside me in the hospital bed.

"You were shot in the chest, and the bullet grazed your lung. Due to the emergency team's efforts, you never went into full cardiac arrest, but it was close. Your surgery went well with no serious complications, but you've remained unconscious all this time." The doctor stated bluntly.

"You'll be able to leave the hospital after a week, now that you're awake. You have a long recovery ahead, but you should be back to normal, more or less, within several months."

I nodded, and the doctor left the room.

"Are you okay?" I asked her.

She laughed. "You're so concerned about me; you're the one who got shot. I'm fine. Now that you're back."

I smiled. "Took me long enough."

"What was it like?" She asked.

I shook my head slowly. "I don't know... It's so... Blank." I cocked my head in thought. "Did you play music for me?"

She nodded. "I played songs I thought you would like."

"I think they guided me back to you."

She cupped my face and kissed me softly. She tasted like something I couldn't live without.

"Did Kanye get the guy?" I asked after the kiss.

She grimaced. "Yes. He... Well, Kanye is on administrative leave pending an investigation now."

"Why?"

"When he caught the shooter, he nearly beat him to death. Other officers had to pull him off and arrest the guy."

"What? Why did he..." I trailed off.

Amanda shrugged. "Kiya is in a psychology class; she thinks it's because he felt guilty about how he treated you in school. He took it out on the guy who shot you. His form of recompense."

"Huh." I absorbed it. "How is Kiya?"

She paused for a fraction of a second, barely noticeable. Then, she spoke. "She's great. Well, all things considered. I took a sabbatical, and she became Gordon's assistant while he's filling in for me. She's going to college for business, so it works well."

"Oh hell yeah. Is she doing as good as I did?"

"Better." She smiled softly.

I laughed.

"Mark..." She paused, contemplating how to bring up what she wanted to say. "While you were here, I took care of your mail and everything with your apartment. I kept your rent up to date." She hesitated. "Your car is missing. Then... One day..."

She gingerly exited the bed and gracefully stepped back onto the floor. She walked over to the chair and picked up her purse.

"This came in the mail. I had to sign for it." She pulled a small, carved ebony box from her purse. "I didn't open it..."

"It came!" I exclaimed. "Open it. Please."

She looked at me with tears in her eyes. She slowly lifted the lid. She burst into tears and covered her mouth with her other hand.

I beamed. "Did it come out good?"

She turned the box to show me. Inside was a large black ring. I had chosen to forgo an expensive diamond, instead using the funds I'd receive from the Corvette to pay for a bespoke jeweler to handcraft the ring. The shape was an intricate, delicate, and elegant crown, with five large rubies completing its geometry. The metal was dipped in black rhodium and glimmered, perfectly complementing Amanda's hair and aesthetic.

"Do you like it?" I asked.

She nodded fiercely, unable to speak.

The door opened, and Kiya entered the room. She wore a white blouse, a black business skirt, and a matching coat. She was holding a stack of papers and a black leather briefcase.

"Hey Amanda, we can't figure out—" Her eyes snapped to me where I sat in bed.

"Mark?!" She screamed.

"Hey, sweetie. It's so good to see you."

"Mark! Amanda—" Her expression grew panicked, and she looked over to Amanda, who nodded and took a deep breath.

"Kiya. Tell him." She whispered.

"Tell me what?" I interjected.

"Mark..." Kiya walked toward me. "I'm pregnant. We're having a baby." Happy tears welled in her eyes. "You're going to be a real Daddy."

The End of Book One. Thank you for taking this journey with me, and I sincerely hope you enjoyed it.

–Deep Rest

Support the author directly and get early access to this continuing story at www.patreon.com/deeprestwriting[1]

Read Book Two: How To Be A Trophy Husband for free at www.reddit.com/u/Specialist-Trip1667/s/nDtV8eBcDY[2]

www.allmylinks.com/deeprest[3]

---

1. http://www.patreon.com/deeprestwriting
2. http://www.reddit.com/u/Specialist-Trip1667/s/nDtV8eBcDY

www.ingramcontent.com/pod-product-compliance
Lightning Source LLC
LaVergne TN
LVHW040826100525
810915LV00007B/96